THE ASTRONAUT'S WIFE

JOE MORTON   CLEA DUVALL

NEW LINE CINEMA PRESENTS A MAD CHANCE PRODUCTION A RAND RAVICH FILM JOHNNY DEPP   CHARLIZE THERON "THE ASTRONAUT'S WIFE"

COSTUME DESIGNER ISIS MUSSENDEN   MUSIC BY GEORGE S. CLINTON   EDITED BY STEVE MIRKOVICH, A.C.E.   TIM ALVERSON   PRODUCTION DESIGNER JAN ROELFS   DIRECTOR OF PHOTOGRAPHY ALLEN DAVIAU, A.S.C.

EXECUTIVE PRODUCERS MARK JOHNSON   BRIAN WITTEN   DONNA LANGLEY   PRODUCED BY ANDREW LAZAR   WRITTEN AND DIRECTED BY RAND RAVICH   CO-PRODUCER DIANA POKORNY

www.astronautswife.com   aol keyword: astronaut

THE ASTRONAUT'S WIFE

ROBERT TINE

Based upon the motion picture screenplay
written by Rand Ravich

St. Martin's Paperbacks

THE ASTRONAUT'S WIFE

Copyright © 1999 by New Line Productions, Inc.
Cover artwork copyright © 1999 by New Line Productions, Inc.

ISBN: 0-312-97018-8

Printed in the United States of America

St. Martin's Paperbacks edition / August 1999

St. Martin's Paperbacks are published by St. Martin's Press, 175 Fifth Avenue, New York, NY 10010.

10 9 8 7 6 5 4 3 2 1

Prologue

There were times when Jillian Armacost felt as if she didn't have a life—not a real one. It was more that she and her husband were controlled by, and were wholly owned subsidiaries of, a government agency. In this case it was the one that one Americans seemed to love and trust above all others: the National Aeronautics and Space Administration—NASA—that crew-cut, square-jawed, can-do, *Houston-we-have-a-problem* organization. Of all the government offspring that Americans mistrusted, they mistrusted NASA the least.

And it took a lot of work to win that trust. If NASA was an old-fashioned movie studio, then the astronauts were the stars, their wives the contract players. Each of them was bound by ironclad contracts—contracts that put the interest of NASA ahead of anything else. On the face of things, this was the case—at least, it was certainly the case with the astronauts themselves. They had worked hard to get to where they were, climbing the steep and slippery military ladder as fliers for the Marine Corps, the United States Navy, and the U.S. Air Force. To have achieved flight status for NASA put you at the top of the heap; it marked you as the best, not just in the armed forces of the United States of America, but as the best in the world. And *this* crop of fliers was said to be the best *ever*.

Spencer Armacost was part of this and, on the face of things, his wife Jillian imagined that he gave himself over to the spirit of NASA completely. But sometimes she caught a look in his eyes, a slight frown, a tiny gesture that suggested that sometimes he hadn't quite been able to bring himself to buy the whole NASA story. They were married, they were exceptionally close. But she could never bring herself to ask Spencer about it. It would have been too much like treason.

Fred Astaire was singing about trouble coming.

All this is not to suggest that Spencer Armacost was your typical bleeding-NASA-blue flier. He knew enough to know a stupid order when he heard one, he knew that NASA was more than likely to make a mistake—and he knew it long before the *Challenger* disaster claimed the lives of six astronauts and the civilian Christa McAuliffe.

Fred Astaire continued, singing about moonlight and love.

Spencer was a thoughtful, well-read man with a passion for flying. He was also the only member of the next shuttle mission who knew anything at all about the career of Fred Astaire—a fact which set him well apart from his fellow fliers who tended to have more red-meat tastes in movies. If they ever saw movies at all, that is.

Fred Astaire was concluding: the only thing to do was dance.

Jillian and Spencer were sprawled in their big bed and you could read the history of that short evening in the archeology of the debris spread around them. On the floor, at the base of the bed was an empty bottle of *pinot noir* and two stemmed glasses, both drained to the dregs. Next to them were some simple white-and-blue pasta bowls, a few strands of spaghettini nestled in a pool of sauce at the bottom. Closer to the bed was a pair of men's pants, bunched and snarled as if they had been hastily kicked off; nearby, as light as a small sheet of gossamer, a pair of pearl-colored women's panties.

The languor of the couple in their bed, their limbs intertwined, told the rest of the story. Their eyes were soft and tired as they watched the movie, their faces lit by the flickering of the television set, the black-and-white movie washing their skin a pale blue. And they stared at it fixedly, as if as long as the movie ran they could keep the real world at bay for a few more moments.

Fred Astaire and Ginger Rogers danced a vigorous *pas de deux* on the deck of a Hollywood-class battleship as chorus boys dressed as grizzled old salts danced behind them.

Spencer shifted slightly but kept his eyes on the television set. "You know," he said, "this flies in the face of everything I know about the United States Navy . . .''

His wife smiled and ran her fingers through his hair. ''Is that so? Too bad you didn't join up.''

Spencer stretched. ''Well, this was made in 1936 or '37—before the big build up for the Second World War. I guess the Navy was just different back then.''

''I guess everything changed after Pearl Harbor,'' Jillian said, laying back on her pillow. ''There's nothing like a sneak attack from a hostile foreign power to ruin a good fleet song-and-dance routine. Wouldn't you say?''

''Uh-huh.'' But it seemed that her husband had lost interest in the joke. His eyes were locked on the screen of the television set with more intensity than a light bit of fluff musical like the Astaire-Rogers musical *Follow the Fleet* would seem to require. It was as if he was hearing the music and the words, seeing the images for the first time and was completely enchanted by them.

Jillian, by contrast, looked less than pleased. ''I hate this part,'' she said.

Spencer looked away from the television screen long enough to shoot a quick glance at his wife. Then his eyes flicked back to the screen. The whole gesture had taken no more than a split second. ''This part?'' he said. ''This part is the best part . . .'' He added his own voice to Fred Astaire's, matching him word for word, phrase for phrase.

Jillian put out a soft hand and touched his face, turning him to face her. She looked him in the eye. "No," she said softly. "That's not what I mean . . . It's this part"—she gestured weakly with her hands as if encompassing the entire room— "this part right now. The part right before you leave. I know you're still here but I know you are leaving, too. I hate this . . ."

Spencer leaned over and kissed his wife softly on the forehead. "I'll call you."

Jillian half smiled and slapped at him weakly. "Don't you dare tease me, Spencer Armacost."

It stood between them like an unbridgeable moat—the mission, Spencer's next foray into space in the space shuttle *Victory*, the latest and most technologically advanced spacecraft in history. On one hand, on a rational level, Jillian could understand the importance of the *Victory* missions in the professional and even the spiritual life of her husband. To be a crew member of the space shuttle was considered the absolute epitome of a military flier's career.

Spencer Armacost had attained these lofty heights by dint of hard work and innate exceptional skill; he was the first to acknowledge, however, that his climb to the top had been facilitated by the deft diplomacy of his beautiful and thoughtful wife. Skill counted for a large part of the equation that added up to a shuttle pilot, but the right wife—the kind of wife who could charm a strategically placed general or thaw the purse strings gripped in the hands of a doubting senator—did not hurt.

The object of the game was to get Spencer a

place on the shuttle crew and Jillian Armacost had worked assiduously to see that he got it. But once the goal had been achieved, she found that the slightest bud of resentment had taken root somewhere deep inside her.

To the average American television viewer, watching a three-second clip of a shuttle launch—usually the seventh or eighth item on the evening news—these expensive excursions into space had gotten to be rather routine. The layman had little understanding or interest in just what went on up there, but the missions, which always seemed to have something to do with satellites, were generally judged to be Good Things For America: it was prestigious and, it was said, those satellites did everything from improving television reception to giving the United States a series of all-seeing eyes high above the earth.

But there was another side to these missions that the man or woman in the street never heard about, probably never even considered. There was a spiritual side to these immense journeys, an otherworldliness as hallowed as any Christian pilgrimage or Muslim hadj. The men who went *out there*, beyond the very confines of the earth, were forever marked by the experience. So few people had actually undergone the process, the shared pool of firsthand knowledge was so tiny, that no one who had not actually done it could possibly understand the significance, could ever appreciate the experience.

And so it was for Jillian and Spencer Armacost.

She dutifully sent her husband off to space—a place she could never follow—and when he returned he was still her husband. But he was always slightly different, as if he knew secrets now—secrets he could never share with her or with any of the uninitiated. It was a tiny, small brother- and sisterhood, one which excluded the vast majority of the population. A Russian cosmonaut, grimy and exhausted after six long months on the Russian space station *Mir* had more in common with Spencer Armacost than Jillian could ever hope to have.

These complex feelings she rendered down to their most simple parts. "I miss you so much when you're gone," Jillian said with a sigh. "It's horrible. I never get a full night's sleep."

Spencer nodded and mussed her short blond hair. "I miss you, too, Jill. Last time we were up, Streck said that if I bellyached about you one more minute, he was going to toss my ass off the ship." Spencer smiled crookedly. "I don't *think* he would really have done it . . . Someone would be bound to notice that I went up but somehow failed to make the trip down."

Jillian harumphed. "You can tell Streck that your ass is mine and he can keep his hands off it, thank you very much."

"Aye, aye, ma'am. Understood," said Spencer briskly. "I will see to it that the commander is given the orders as to the disposition of my ass post haste, ma'am."

Alex Streck was Spencer's immediate superior and mission commander. Both he and his wife Natalie were good friends of the Armacosts, despite slight differences in age and the subtle distinctions of rank.

"Good," said Jillian with a little laugh. She snuggled in closer, burrowing under his arm and pushing up against his body, as if to absorb warmth from it. "My class wants you to come in when you get back. I think they only tolerate me to get to you." Jillian Armacost was being unduly modest. She was a wildly popular second grade teacher at a local Florida elementary school. Though she did have to admit that having a husband who was an astronaut with flight status probably gave her a little edge when it came to engaging her boisterous and rambunctious pack of second graders.

Spencer stretched in the bed. "I might be able to arrange a visit," he said cagily, like a gambler trying to make the most of a less than perfect hand. "It'll take a little bit of doing, though," he added.

"What will it take?" Jillian asked.

"Well, it wouldn't hurt for you to be a little nice to me," said Spencer, smiling.

"How nice?" Jillian asked, as if weighing her chips before she bet anything.

"Oh, you know," said Spencer airily. "You know me . . . I'm just an old married man, a little kindness goes quite a long way with an old coot like me."

Jillian brushed her lips against his and reached down under the sheet, her hand closing around what she discovered there. Jillian's eyes went wide, as if

she were the virginal heroine of a nineteenth-
century novel.

"Why, Mr. Armacost, whatever do you have
there?"

Spencer said through a stiff upper lip, "Why,
Mrs. Armacost, whatever do you mean?"

As they melted into each other's arms, Fred
Astaire's singing of music and dance provided the
only possible answer.

1

The firm and authoritative voice came through a crackling cloud of static.

"*Victory*, we are at T-minus thirty-one seconds, your onboard computers are functioning. Start auto sequence."

Mission Control was talking to the space shuttle *Victory*. The great pile of vehicle was standing straight up on the launch pad, ready to blast off and head for space. The whole machine was made up of several components: the familiar and elegant winged orbiter, two solid rocket boosters, and a giant external tank.

Despite all the talk about onboard computers, for the next few minutes the *Victory* would be dealing with a technology as complicated as an ordinary bottle rocket. Spencer and Alex Streck and the rest of the crew were strapped into the orbiter fifteen stories above the ground, the larger portion of which was stuffed with hundred of tons of volatile fuel. In a moment or two, someone would set fire to it and they would be on their way.

The voice of Mission Control seemed to pervade the very air of the Cape. Jillian Armacost had been through it so many times she could imagine every order, every check, every response as they went over the air between Mission Control and the shuttle itself.

Jillian stood at the open French windows of her house. Far on the horizon, thrusting up into the blue of a Florida morning sky like a skyscraper, was the shuttle and the ugly steel fretwork of the attendant gantry. She stared out through the humid air, not quite able to believe that her beloved husband was strapped into a seat atop that strange, rather alien contraption.

The countdown to liftoff had started and was well along. Jillian could imagine the voice. *"T-minus 14, 13, 12, 11 . . ."*

Suddenly Jillian felt a chill and she wrapped her arms around herself. She trembled slightly.

"Ten, ignition on. T-minus 9, 8, 7 . . ."

From far off came the sound of a low rumbling. *"Six . . . Engine start . . ."* The rumbling grew in intensity as the sound waves moved across the flat landscape.

"Four, 3, 2, 1. Zero and liftoff . . ."

The window in front of Jillian vibrated slightly as the sound ricocheted off the thin panes. She reached and touched the trembling glass, as if connecting herself to the sound connected her to the craft quivering on the horizon. It was as if the shuttle was anxious to be gone, desperate to shake off the bounds of tiresome gravity.

Spencer spoke for the first time. *"Mission Control, this is* Victory. *We have left the pad . . ."* It was a remarkably prosaic way of saying that tons of volatile fuel were burning up, pushing another huge hunk of metal into the sky.

"Roger that, Victory," Mission Control responded. *"You are go for throttle up . . ."*

"Mission Control," Spencer answered, *"we have throttle up. It is a fine day for flying, Houston . . ."*

Jillian watched as the shuttle emerged from the vast blizzard of smoke, its snub nose pointed straight toward the sky. No matter how many times Jillian had seen a launch, this great eruption of smoke and steel, she always felt that the module rose out of the dramatic upheaval slowly and tentatively, as if straining to make it into the sky like a weak fledgling new from the nest. It seemed to move so slowly that she half expected the entire contraption to fall over, sloping to one side like a tottering drunk, unable to stand the forces of staying upright for another second. She did not know she was holding her breath, but she was.

Two minutes into the flight, the boosters were used up and separated from the craft. While they appeared to float gracefully away from the main body of the vessel, the separation was actually a gut-wrenching yank that no matter how many times Spencer felt it, it seemed as if the whole ship was being ripped apart. You never got used it.

"Mission Control, we are standing by for SRB separation," said Spencer, bracing himself for what came next.

Even worse than that first separation, though, was the next phase of the flight which came a mere six minutes later. After about eight minutes of flight the shuttle was shaken by a terrifying explosion, and the huge external tank separated from the main body of the vessel.

"Separation confirmed," said Spencer. The trim of the vessel changed dramatically. It seemed to have been shot out of a sling, picking up speed at a dramatic rate as it lost weight. "Houston, we are at eighteen thousand knots and accelerating."

The fire was blinding. The roaring of the engines deafening. The sky had changed in color, from dark blue, then pale, then darkness. Houston came up: "You are go for main engine shut-off."

Abruptly the overwhelming roar of the engines vanished and there was no sound. No sound at all. The silence was so complete and so sudden you could almost feel it.

The silence was pierced for a moment or two as Alex Streck fired short burns from the shuttle's pair of maneuvering engines. Those small blasts pushed the craft over the momentous hump, the amazing transition from earth to space.

Spencer's voice was conversational in tone, as if he had nothing more important to announce than what was for lunch. "We have main engine shut-off," Spencer calmly informed Mission Control. "We are now in orbit . . ."

Jillian spun the globe. The orb whirled around, the countries and the oceans blending together until the whole world seemed to be a multi-colored mass. Then she put her hand out and stopped it abruptly. She looked around the room and down at the bright faces of her second grade class. Twenty-four boys and girls stared back at her, each one hanging on her every word.

"What do they have in Kansas?" Jillian asked. Instantly, there was a chorus of voices responding to her question.

"*Corn*!"

Jillian thought for a moment to think of another question. "And what do they have in . . . Georgia?"

"*Peaches*!" the class answered instantly.

Jillian jabbed a tiny portion of the globe. "And what do we have right here in Florida?" she asked.

Everyone in the class responded with alacrity. "We have oranges in Florida!"

Well, all but one said that. A lone little boy answered, "We have rocket ships!" His eyes were bright at the very thought of such magical contraptions.

Jillian smiled at her space-obsessed pupil. "Yes, Calvin, oranges *and* rocket ships."

Just then the door of the classroom opened and young girl, a child a little older than the pupils in Jillian Armacost's class, came bustling, bursting with self-importance, into the room.

"What is it, Lynne?" Jillian asked.

"Mrs. Whitfield sent me here with a message for you," the girl said excitedly. Mrs. Whitfield was the formidable principal of the elementary school.

"What's the message?"

"Mrs. Armacost, you got a phone call!"

Phone calls at school were so out of the ordinary daily routine of the day that it was with a mixture of apprehension tinged with a distinct sense of curiosity about who might be calling her in the middle of the working day.

The secretaries in the school office were full of inquiring looks, consumed, as Jillian was, by curiosity.

She picked up the phone. "Hello?"

The response was a man's voice, a voice she did not recognize. "Is that Mrs. Armacost?"

"Yes," she said, her heart sinking. She knew the voice of NASA when she heard it. She could not help but wonder if something terrible had happened to her husband. "Yes, this is Jillian Armacost."

Jillian had guessed correctly. "This is NASA communications," said the man. "We have your husband for you."

The man made it all sound so simple, as if he was putting through a call from somewhere nearby—across town maybe—as opposed to from high up in outer space.

Jillian felt a tremor of excitement flash through her body. "You . . . you have my what?"

"Stay on the line please . . ."

There was a crackle of static on the line, then Jillian heard the man say, "Go ahead, Commander."

There was another burst of static, as if the atmosphere was clearing its throat, then to Jillian's astonishment, she heard Spencer's voice come on the line. "Jillian? Are you there?"

Jillian seemed even more surprised than she had been a moment before. "Spencer? Is that you?"

"Can you hear me?" It was definitely Spencer's voice, but there was an aerated, hollow quality to it, as if they were on a very long distance call. Which, Jillian thought, was exactly what they were doing.

"Spencer, I can't believe this," Jillian exclaimed. "How did this happen?"

Through the ether, Jillian heard her husband laugh. The sound made her shiver with delight. "I told you I'd call you," he said, continuing to chuckle. "It's amazing isn't it."

As if to compensate for the immense distance, Jillian could only shout into the phone, her voice seeming to ring through the entire school building. "Yes, amazing," she yelled.

There was a moment of silence as they listened to their connection, each straining to hear the other breathe.

Finally Spencer broke the silence. And he did it in a typically Spencer fashion. "Hey, Jill?"

"Yes?"

"Tell me something. It's really important, okay?" There was a note of urgency in his voice that sent her levels of anxiety skyrocketing once again.

"Yes, Spencer," she said nervously. "What is it?"

"You have to tell me . . ."

"Yes?"

"What are you wearing?" She could hear the laughter in his voice and she wanted to slap him and kiss him at the same time. "I have to know, Jillian."

"Spencer . . ." said Jillian reprovingly, as if she was threatening one of her little students with a time-out.

"Come on," Spencer replied, "no one else is listening . . . C'mon, tell me. It's just you and me."

An apologetic-sounding male voice broke in on the line. "Uh, not exactly, Commander," he said a touch sheepishly. "Including Houston and Jet Propulsion Labs, there are about three hundred folks on the line just at the moment."

Spencer ignored the caution. "Jillian, are you wearing that black skirt of yours? The tight one?"

In spite of being embarrassed Jillian laughed loudly. "Settle down, cowboy. This is a school teacher you're talking to, you know?"

Spencer laughed and paused a moment before continuing. "Nice day down there, huh?" he asked. "Not a cloud in the sky, right? One of those perfect Florida days . . ."

"It's beautiful here," said Jillian. Then a weird sort of dread overcame her, a panicky feeling that needed to be quelled immediately. He had spoken so wistfully about something so mundane, so work-aday, so *not* Spencer. Why would he be interested in the weather? It was as if he was asking her about something he would never see again, something deep in his past

"Spencer," she asked quickly, "where are you?"

Before he could answer, the voice of officialdom, the NASA voice, came back on the line abruptly. "Thirty seconds to go, Commander," he cautioned.

Jillian felt her panic ratchet up a notch. "Spencer, where exactly are you?"

There was a pause, the briefest delay. It could have been due to the distance of transmission, it could have been reluctance on Spencer's part. Jillian did not know. She did not care. The hesitation had not lasted a second, not a half second, but it seemed to Jillian to have played out over an hour or more.

"Can you see outside, Jill?" he asked finally.

"Yes, Spencer." Jillian glanced out of the window in the office. The day was bright and sunny, the sky blue, just as her husband had described it to her a few moments before.

"Fifteen seconds, Commander," said the guy from Houston.

"Jillian . . ." said Spencer wistfully. "I am right above you. Right over you now."

Jillian knew it was foolish, but she couldn't stop herself. Without thinking about it she pulled the phone cord as far as it would go to the farthest extension of the wire. Then she threw open the window and looked into the sky.

"You looking up?" Spencer asked.

"Ten seconds, Commander . . ."

"Jillian, smile for me, huh? Okay?"

Jillian gazed into the sky, a smile on her face, but with tears in the corner of her eyes. "I already am."

"Five seconds, Commander Armacost." You could almost see the guy with his eyes glued to the digital clock on his console, counting off the seconds.

"Jillian, I—" That was all he managed to say before his voice was lost in a sea of static.

"Spencer?" Jillian sounded as if she was *demanding* that her husband not leave her.

"I'm sorry, Mrs. Armacost," said the voice of NASA. "We lost the link. But he's talking to Mission Control right now. Everything is fine. We'll take good care of him." That was NASA all over, don't worry, your kindly old uncle is here, always on the job, taking care of the boys up there in space.

"Thank you," Jillian whispered. "I know you will."

2

Jillian could never quite reconcile herself to the
term space *travel*. It wasn't travel as human beings
understood the word; it wasn't as if Spencer was
just another husband away on an extended business
trip. There was something about his going into
space that made his absence seem more extreme,
bizarre—almost unnatural. And attendant on these
peculiar circumstances, the anxiety and fear that Jillian felt was that much more acute. And while it
was possible to forget your husband for a moment
or two when he's at a sales conference in Santa Fe
or a convention in San Diego, his actions, his fate
was ever with her when Spencer was in space. A
slight vibration of apprehension, slightly flustering
like a low-grade fever, was always with her. When
Spencer was away, up there, it was as if he had
died but he was going to come back to life, as if
resurrection was guaranteed by NASA and the
United States government, as well as by God and
all the saints.

She could not be alone—not for the whole time he was gone. When Spencer was away, Jillian turned to her younger sister Nan for companionship and a steady guiding hand. Not that Nan was all that reliable in the conduct of her own life, but she had an instinctive knowledge of what her big sister needed when Spencer was away. And Jillian was glad to have her near.

Of course, like many siblings close in age they were a study in contrasts. Jillian was thoughtful and took care of the things that were precious in her life, constantly giving thought to the results and possible aftermath of even trivial occurrences; Nan, of course, was impulsive and spontaneous, wandering in and out of jobs, friendships, and relationships with men, without much thought for the future or the consequences.

And although they were sisters they could not have looked more dissimilar. Both were pretty, but Jillian had finer, more classically even features which were set off by her soft, short blond hair and her wide blue eyes. Nan's face was small, and its component parts were pleasingly out of of proportion. Her eyes were just a tiny bit too far apart, her mouth slightly off kilter, her hair was a rather random mop of brown silk. All of this imperfection served to make her a pretty young woman.

There was a haphazardness to her gamine face that suggested a mischievousness that contrasted with her sister's alternating moods of serenity and anxiety.

The two women dressed in completely different

manners and styles as well. Jillian kept things casual and classical, never straying an inch beyond the boundaries of good taste; Nan looked thrown together.

She appeared for dinner at Jillian's door that night dressed in bright pants, a ribbed knit shirt, a pair of black classic Keds on her feet. Had she looked any more current she would have been dressing in the styles of the week after next.

The two sisters were at work in the Armacost kitchen, back to back, preparing dinner. Even the tasks the two chose to do pointed up the differences between them. Jillian was bent over a cutting board, chef's knife in hand, carefully but skillfully making a julienne of fresh vegetables. Nan, no less skillfully, worked the cork out of a bottle of red wine. Behind them, mounted under the glass-fronted kitchen cabinets, a small color television set played, the sound off. The sisters were hardly aware that it was there.

"Let me get this straight . . . he called you from space?" said Nan as she eased the cork from the bottle of *pinot noir*. She sounded incredulous. Despite her sister's marriage to an astronaut she still could not get used to this NASA stuff. It was still science fiction to her. Of course, it wasn't the technology involved that astonished her, but the act itself. Nan was not famous for her success with men.

The cork emerged with a pop. "From outer space," she repeated as she reached for a wine glass.

Jillian, still engaged with her vegetables, did not

turn around. But she nodded, as if to herself. "Well, technically not outer space," she said. "He was still in the earth's orbit. But, yes, he called me from the orbiter. Out there." She gestured vaguely toward the window with the knife in her right hand.

Nan sighed and sipped her wine. "I can't get Stanley to call from the Beef and Brew and you get a call from outer space. You gotta admit, that's got to make a kid feel a little . . . inadequate." She poured a glass of the scarlet wine and handed it to Jillian. "Not that it's your fault or anything, Jilly-o . . ."

Jillian smiled and took the glass. She thought that if she was in Nan's shoes she would not exactly relish the idea of a call from Nan's latest boyfriend, Stanley, whether from the Beef and Brew, outer space, or anywhere else. Stanley, sadly, was no woman's idea of a knight in shining armor.

"Like I said," Jillian replied gently, "technically it wasn't outer space, Nan."

Nan shrugged and shook her head. "Earth's orbit, outer space, Jupiter, whatever. Jill, if you want to get really technical about things, you scored." She took a deep pull on her wine and shook her head again. "Oh man . . ."

"What?" Jillian asked.

"I don't get it," Nan replied. "How is it—we grow up in the same house, we watched the same television shows, ate the same frozen dinners . . . Your background is no different than mine, you know. It's no nature versus nurture thing here.

We weren't separated at birth or anything like that—''

Jillian looked puzzled, not quite sure where her sister was going with this. "So what?"

Nan rolled her eyes and swigged a bit more wine. "So what? So *you* land Johnny Rocket Boy—who probably would have sent you flowers from outer space if he could have—and I keep on ending up with subtly different models of 'throws up on himself Elmo.' " She took another gulp of the wine and then winked slyly at her sister. "And let me guess . . . I'll bet he's good at the little things, too, isn't he?"

"What little things?" Jillian asked innocently. Her eyes were bright and she was smiling broadly, but she could not match her sister for brazenness. After a moment, she blushed and looked away, turning back to her vegetables.

"Those little things that mean so much," said Nan, peering at her sister over the top of her wine glass. "You know what I'm talking about, Jilly."

"Maybe," she replied and blushed a little bit more.

Nan laughed out loud at the truth she read in her sister's eyes. "It's true," she said. "Men are like parking spaces. The good ones are taken and you can bet that the available ones are all handicapped. Maybe *you* don't know that, but *I* sure as hell do."

The two sisters shared a laugh over that, Jillian shaking her head ruefully as she expertly diced a zucchini. "There's a man out there for you, Nan. Give it time."

"How much time is time," Nan shot back. "Wait a minute, Jilly-o . . . I know . . . Maybe, just maybe, I'm gay. Maybe that's it. I could be gay, you know."

"Oh, Nan, you? You are not the type."

"Maybe I could get to like it," Nan countered. "You know, gay is pretty damn cool these days . . . or is that over already." She considered that for a moment. "No, I think it's still pretty cool."

"Nan, stop it!"

But Nan wouldn't stop it. She knew that anything that took her sister's mind off of the space mission was good for her. "What? You don't think I could be gay? I could be gay. I know if I really tried . . ." Nan stood up straight squaring her shoulders against some formidable challenge. "Okay, Jillian, that's it. It's official. You have a gay sister. From now on I want you to—" Then she yelped in alarm. "Jesus Christ, Jillian! Be careful."

Nan was gaping at her sister's slim hands. The silver blade of the chef's knife had sliced deep into her left index finger. Blood was spilling out among the green and yellow of the vegetables.

But Jillian did not appear to have noticed.

"What?" Nan yelped. "Jill, what?"

Jill did not respond. Rather, she was staring at the mute screen of the television set. Nan followed the line of her gaze and saw still pictures of two men, two men identified by the television network as Commander Spencer Armacost and Captain Alex

Streck. At the top of the screen were the words: *Special News Report.*

For a moment time seemed arrested. There was no sound. There was no movement. It was as if for that split second both women had become as still and as inert as statues, their bones and joints frozen. The spell on Jill broke first.

"Oh my God . . ." Jillian gasped. Then she pushed past Nan to raise the volume on the television set. But she was a second too late. They had missed the story.

". . . this has been a special report," said the deep-voiced announcer. "We now return you to the program already in progress." In a matter of seconds a midday talk show blared from the screen.

"Jill! What's going on?" Nan yelled.

Jillian did not answer. She twisted the knob on the set, running madly through the channels, but there was nothing more about her husband, just regular programming—the game shows, the cooking shows, the soap operas seeming all the more inane when contrasted against the dread that had suddenly filled her body.

"Jill? Jilly?" said Nan. Jillian did not appear to have heard. She was still desperately turning the channels when the doorbell chimed. Both Jillian and Nan froze.

Jillian knew exactly what was happening. "Oh God," she whispered. "It's them."

"It's who?" demanded Nan.

"NASA . . . they probably have a trauma team or an honor guard or something. This is it."

"Jill, you don't know—"

But Jill had raced to the front door and thrown it open. Standing on the step was a middle-aged man in a well-cut gray suit—the NASA uniform—and with a particularly sheepish look on his face. He seemed to have trouble looking Jillian square in the eye and he shuffled his feet nervously.

Jill had met most of the *Victory* team at one time or another, but she had never seen this man before. In her fear and anxiety she felt a deep, irrational loathing for this anonymous man, a warm body on whom she could vent her wrath.

"Who are you?" she demanded.

"I'm Sherman Reese, Mrs. Armacost," he said softly. "I'm from NASA. It's about your husband."

Jillian's anger had flared up for a moment and now had burned itself out. She slumped against the door frame, her pretty face pale and drawn as if the last few minutes of her life had exhausted her, had drained her of her entire reserves of energy and strength. Blood was dripping from her finger like a leaky faucet.

"What has happened?" she asked. Her throat was tight, her voice harsh and dry.

"We'd like you to come down to the—" Reese started, but was interrupted.

From inside the house Nan shouted, "*Jill—there's something on TV about Spencer!*"

"We have a car waiting," said Sherman Reese softly. He took her arm gently, as if to guide her toward it.

"Jill?" Nan called from inside the house. "Jilly, I think you better come and see—"

As if suddenly afraid of Reese, Jill backed away, as if by not seeing him she could turn back the clock by those few minutes needed to set the world right again. There would be no NASA man at her door, no sinister NASA car in her driveway.

"Please, Mrs. Armacost," said Reese quietly. "Captain Streck's wife is already over there. Any questions you have will be answered down at the—"

Jillian turned and ran back into the house, Reese following in her footsteps.

"Mrs. Armacost, please don't make this more difficult than it is already." Jillian vanished into the kitchen. It was here that Reese found her, gazing at the television set while Nan wrapped Jillian's sliced opened finger.

"Mrs. Armacost," said Reese, "the Director wants . . ."

"Shush," said Jillian. She did not even so much as glance in his direction.

There was a reporter on the television set, microphone in hand, standing in front of the chain-link gate at the security checkpoint at the entrance to the Cape. It was odd that the reporter would be doing his standup from outside the complex; there was an elaborate press room inside the space administration building. It could only mean that there had been a complete press lockdown on the story.

The television correspondent more or less confirmed the suspicion. "All we know for sure—and we don't know much—is that both men were outside the orbiter, performing repairs on a communication satellite. The condition of Armacost and Streck, as well as the well-being of the rest of the shuttle crew, is unknown at this time . . ."

While the reporter signed off and threw the story back to the network, Jillian turned to Reese and looked him square in the eye. Her voice was eerily calm.

"Is my husband dead?" she asked.

Reese shook his head apologetically. "Ma'am, I'm afraid I don't know anything about the condition of your husband. I have been sent here by the Director to—"

"Is my husband dead?" Jilly asked again, her voice edged with a tinge of hysteria, as if the false calm was melting away and she was just barely holding on to her feelings.

Reese shrugged. "To be honest, ma'am, I just don't know. Details are very sketchy."

"If you don't know," Jillian said coldly, "take me to someone who does. Now."

She looked at the man's starched shirt, as stiff and as spotless an officer's whites, his crisp perfectly cut suit, that smooth shave, and the shine on his shoes and felt contempt for him. He was down here whole and healthy while her husband was deep in space, far beyond rescue, dead in the silence of space.

Reese shrugged. "That's what I'm here to do, Mrs. Armacost. Captain Streck's wife is already there."

Nan grabbed her sister roughly by the sleeve and
tugged her toward the door. "Come on, Jilly, let's
get over and there and find out what the hell is
going on."

Sherman Reese stepped between then. "I'm
sorry," he said, sounding as if he were *genuinely*
sorry. "I only have security clearance for Mrs. Armacost."

"Then you better get security clearance for Mrs.
Armacost's sister, mister, because—"

Reese looked beseechingly at Jillian. "Please,
Mrs. Armacost, could you tell your sister—"

Jillian nodded and tried to stand straight. It was
odd; she did not feel the desire to cry—not yet,
anyway. She turned to Nan.

"It'll be okay, Nan," she said, keeping her voice
as steady as possible. "I'll be okay."

"You sure?" Nan's eyes narrowed.

"I'm sure . . ."

The radio was on in the no-frills government car
that carried them through the quiet suburb.

"NASA is now officially confirming that Commander Spencer Armacost and Captain Alex Streck
were outside of the space shuttle *Victory* when there
was an explosion on the communication satellite on
which they were doing repairs . . ."

Reese looked worried as the words spilled out of
the radio, but the young woman did not appear to
be listening to the grim report. Rather, she was engrossed in the world beyond the window of the car.

It was a fine Florida summer evening. People were sitting on their lawns, laboring over barbecues, lazing in swimming pools. Kids rode bikes. Life was continuing even as hers might be coming to an end.

3

The fluorescent lights of the bare corridors of NASA headquarters washed any remaining color out of Jillian's face. The only sound was the clip of their footsteps on the white linoleum and the annoying hum from the lights. Jillian was numb and silent. Sherman Reese was silent as well, reserved and speechless the way people are when they are in the presence of tragedy that does not really concern them, not directly anyway—it was the sort of situation that leads people to say, "I don't know what to say."

As they walked the labyrinthine hallways they passed some staff members. Jillian did not know them, but they seemed know who she was—they glanced at her ashen face quickly then looked away just as quickly, as if they were catching a glimpse of a condemned prisoner on her way to the gallows. One or two flashed sympathetic smiles—not at Jillian, but at Reese, none of them envying the grim task of escorting a woman who might or might not

have become a widow in just the last few hours or
so.

It was with some relief that Sherman Reese delivered his charge to her destination. It was another
bare, windowless, fluorescent-lit room, a wide conference table and a set of chairs the only furniture.
On the wall was a monitor showing the activity in
Mission Control. There was no sound coming from
it.

Seated at the table was a lone woman. She was
older than Jillian by a number of years—somewhere in her middle forties—and her pale face was
lined with grief. Jillian knew her well—it was Natalie Streck—but had she not known her from happier times she probably would not have recognized
her now. Her shoulders were slumped, her eyes
dark, red-rimmed, and hollow. She looked as if she
had aged a decade in a matter of minutes.

Jillian rushed to her and threw her arms around
her. "Oh, Jillian," Natalie cried into Jillian's shoulder. "Oh God . . ." Both women gave into their
tears and Sherman Reese stood off to one side, his
hands thrust into his pockets trying to look as if he
wasn't there.

Natalie pulled out of the embrace and looked into
Jillian's face. "They're so far away, Jillian," she
said softly, fighting to keep down her tears. "Alex
and Spencer, Jillian, they are so far away. And
there's nothing we can do for them."

Jillian stroked her hair and rocked her in her
arms as she might a little child. "Shhh, Natalie,
shhhhh. . . ."

"Oh, Jillian. He's dead," Natalie wailed. "I know he's dead. I know he's dead. I can feel it."

Jillian felt herself go cold, as if she had stepped into a freezer. If Alex Streck was dead, then Spencer was dead as well.

"What have they told you?" Jillian asked.

Natalie shot a cold glance at Sherman Reese. "Nothing. They won't tell me anything."

Both women turned on Reese. "Why?" Jillian demanded. "Why haven't we been told anything?"

Reese shrugged and felt useless. "I'm sorry. I have not been authorized to say—"

At that moment, as if on cue, the door to the conference room opened and a man walked in. He was a distinguished-looking white-haired man whom Jillian recognized as the Director, a man she had only met at official functions—a quick handshake, sometimes followed by a photograph, and then the great man passed on.

"Sir," said Reese deferentially and motioned toward the two women like a headwaiter showing a diner to his table, "these are Mrs. Streck and Mrs.—"

"I know who they are, Sherman," the Director said imperiously. "Mrs. Streck, Mrs. Armacost . . . First, let me tell you that your husbands are alive."

Both women felt as if great weights had been lifted from their shoulders.

"Oh, thank God," breathed Natalie Streck.

"They're back on the orbiter now," the Director continued, "and we're going to bring the orbiter down just as soon as we get a window."

"Can we talk to them?" Jillian asked.

The Director shot a look at Reese and then looked back to the two women. He shook his head. "That is not possible, Mrs. Armacost. I am afraid that both Captain Streck and Commander Armacost are unconscious at this time."

"Oh my God," said Natalie Streck. "Are they badly hurt? Are they in pain?"

The Director did not answer the questions directly. He slipped around the questions like a boxer avoiding a punch. "We have an MD on this mission, ma'am, who has done his best to make them comfortable. Furthermore, we are monitoring all their vital signs from down here at Mission Control. They are both stable but, at this time, they remain unconscious."

Vital signs, thought Jillian. That was NASA-speak for her husband's life.

"What happened out there?" She heard her own voice ask a question, and was surprised to hear it.

Once again the Director tried to avoid the question. "All the information we have at our disposal at the moment is extremely sketchy, Mrs. Armacost—unreliable to say the least. I wouldn't want to venture an opinion—"

Jillian was in no mood for obfuscation. "What happened out there?" she snapped, cutting the Director off. The man looked at her with hard eyes for a moment. He was not a man who was used to being interrupted by anyone, least of all an astronaut's wife. Still, there was something in the look on Jillian's face that told him that she would not stand for any circumlocutions on his part.

"Your husbands were outside the orbiter," he said slowly. "It was a perfectly routine task. They were engaged in repairs on a satellite. There was an explosion and . . ." The director looked over at Reese, then back at Natalie and Jillian. "We lost contact with both astronauts . . ." He shifted uncomfortably and looked down at the floor. "We lost contact with both of them for about two minutes."

Jillian's gaze lost none of its intensity. "Two minutes? You lost contact for two minutes?"

The Director continued to look at the floor. Suddenly the buzz from the fluorescent light seemed very loud.

"What do you mean," said Jillian, "lost contact?" There was no doubt in the tone of her voice that she was going to get a straight answer.

The Director glanced at her and then back down at the floor. "They were off radio and out of visual contact" he said. "After the explosion they drifted behind the shuttle. We had to bring the craft around one hundred and eighty degrees to get them."

"They were all alone," said Natalie Streck, her voice shot through with tears. She shivered at the thought of her husband floating alone and hurt in the middle of so much nothingness.

It was plain that the Director had decided that he had heard enough of wifely hysteria. "But now they're back on the shuttle and they will be back down here just as soon as we can manage it," he said briskly. He gestured to Sherman Reese urging him forward. "Mr. Reese here will stay with you until we can take you to your husbands." He changed to a more human pitch. "I've worked closely with both Spencer and Alex, and I know they are both strong and courageous men. I'm sure they are going to be fine. I give you my word."

With that, the Director turned and with a nod to Reese, as if handing the two women officially to his command, left the room. There was a sense that the Director was glad that the interview was over and done with. He had more important things to do.

Natalie and Jillian did not care if the Director had stayed and held their hands. NASA, the space program—none of these weighty matters were of the slightest significance to them now.

"They were all alone out there, Jill," said Natalie tearfully. "They could have been lost forever."

Jillian put her arms around Natalie and held her close. "It will be fine, Natalie. We have to believe that. That's all we can do. Get them back down and get them home. Then everything will be all right. Understand, Natalie?"

Natalie Streck did her best to nod and smile, as if she really believed what her friend had said. She pushed her face hard against Jillian's shoulder, burrowing for comfort.

Sherman Reese pointed to the television monitor mounted on the wall above them. "This monitor will show the view from the shuttle as they land. Would you like me to get the link up? You'll be able to see the whole thing from here."

Neither Natalie nor Jillian heard him; they had

traveled too far into their own grief to care what anyone said to them. There was a very long silence as Reese waited for an answer, for a set of instructions—anything—from the two women. But nothing came—and nothing was going to come from either of them.

"I'll get the link up," said Reese, as if to himself. He got busy doing whatever it was he had to do.

Natalie and Jillian paid no attention. As with the Director, they didn't care about Sherman Reese, either.

4

The space shuttle *Victory* flew noiselessly though the sky, dropping thousands of feet in a matter of seconds until it was over the lush green landscape of Florida.

Jillian watched the vehicle intently while listening to the dispassionate voice of the pilot of the *Victory* reporting from the flight deck of the spacecraft. He was a man that Jillian did not know well and she would not normally have recognized his voice. "Thirty feet at 235 knots. Twenty at 225 . . . ten feet at 220. Eight at 215 . . . five feet at 210 knots . . . almost down now . . . two feet at 200. One foot. Zero. Ground Control, this is *Victory*, we are down."

From somewhere in the building Jillian could hear the sounds of cheers and applause. The pilot, however, was not celebrating—not yet. He still had a very large vehicle traveling at a very great rate of speed to slow down and bring to a stop.

"One hundred and fifty knots," he intoned.

"One hundred knots. Eighty knots. Sixty-five knots, 30, 15, 10 knots . . . We are stopped. Ground Control, this is *Victory*." The voice seemed to lighten slightly. "This is *Victory*, come and get us."

Almost as the words were broadcast a cavalcade of emergency vehicles raced out onto the tarmac strip of the runway, the red and blue lights on their roofs bright and sharp, glancing off the gray of the dawn. There were two ambulances, one each for the injured men, as well as a phalanx of other trucks that Jillian could not identify.

A feed from a news reporter came out of the monitor, as a bulletin was made to network headquarters in New York City.

"*. . . unprecedented actions on the part of NASA to take care of its own. The* Victory *was just a few hundred thousand miles into a three-million-mile mission when the accident occurred and the decision was made almost instantly to cut the mission by eighty percent to bring the injured men home. You have just seen a rare dawn landing of a space shuttle. NASA and the two injured astronauts were lucky that there was a weather window open so soon. It's something of a miracle . . .*"

Jillian's only idea of a miracle had nothing to do with weather windows. The miracle was that her husband had been hurt far out in space and now he was on earth again. Now she wanted to see him, to see for herself just how miraculous this had all been.

The reporter continued. "*The two astronauts, Ar-*

macost and Streck will be medivaced to a hospital facility here on the base..."

The hospital was as calm and as white as the conference room and the same fluorescent hum seemed to have followed Jillian here like a fly she could not get rid of.

Jillian stood at one end of the corridor with the doctor taking care of her husband. At the far end of the corridor stood Natalie Streck with the doctor who was overseeing treatment of Alex. Between the two, in the middle of the corridor, still feeling like a fish out of water, stood Sherman Reese.

Jillian hung on the doctor's every word. He was young and seemed competent—plus he was reporting nothing but good news. Her spirits rose with every word.

"He's breathing on his own," the doctor said. "His vital functions are good and strong. As far as we can tell, there has been no brain damage. It should only be a matter of time before your husband regains consciousness."

Jillian nodded, and then looked down the corridor to Natalie. Her doctor had his hand on her shoulder, and Jillian could tell that the news she was getting was not so good.

"What about Alex?" Jillian asked.

The doctor sighed and looked uncomfortable. "Captain Streck is an older man than your husband. There was a tremendous strain put on his heart..."

Jillian looked down the hall again and caught

Natalie looking back at her, but her eyes were blank with grief.

She had been awake all night, she had been put through an emotional wringer, but nothing would stop her from sitting at Spencer's bedside, a vigil she knew she had to keep.

Spencer lay inert in his bed, an intravenous tube plugged into the crook of his arm, the monotonous drip the only movement in the room. She fought the fatigue as best she could, but gradually her eyes began to close. The narcotic effects of stress and relief flooded into her body and despite her resolve she felt herself giving into sleep. But the instant her eyes closed, she heard a whisper. For a moment, she wondered if she had dreamed it, then she heard it again.

"Jillian?"

Instantly, Jillian's eyes opened wide.

"Jillian?" Spencer sounded unsure of himself, as if not quite certain of her name.

Jillian stood up and went to the bed, leaning over the bed, looking into Spencer's eyes. He looked back, gazing into her eyes, as if reacquainting himself with her perfect features.

Spencer smiled slightly. "I told you . . ." he said groggily. "I told you I'd call."

A great wave of happiness washed through her and she laughed and cried at the same time and threw her arms around him. "Never," she gasped through her tears, "*never* leave me again."

Spencer nodded against the pillow. "I promise," he said with a little smile.

"Never, Spencer," she said, her voice almost stern. "Do you hear me?"

"I promise," he said, trying to raise an arm, as if swearing an oath. "I promise, Jillian. I will never leave you again."

Their faces were close and he raised his head and kissed her, first on the lips and then on the warm corner of her neck, as if learning her contours again, tasting her, savoring the smoothness and smell of her skin. His lips felt electric on her skin.

"Thanks for coming," he said, a little smile on his face. "I mean, I know how you hate hospitals."

This time Jillian laughed out loud, luxuriating in the rapturous delight of his return.

Spencer's face darkened. "How's Alex doing?" he asked. "Is he all right?"

The look on her face told him all he needed to know. "Not good," she said sadly. "The doctors say that there was a terrible strain on his heart."

Spencer seemed to wince in pain and he closed his eyes. "Is Natalie with him?"

Jillian nodded. "Yes. She's there."

Spencer nodded. "That's good," he said. "That's good . . ." Then he seemed to slip into a peaceful sleep.

Alex Streck had been consigned to the Ultra Intensive Care Unit and lay unconscious, inert on the bed. He had more than a simple intravenous tube in his arm. His chest was dotted with pressure pads,

and a bank of machines monitored every breath and
nerve in his body. They whirred and clicked and
beeped softly, mechanical guardians that never
slept.

Natalie Streck, clothed from foot to neck in a
clean suit, slept soundly in a chair at his side. Her
face was gray and lined, her mouth slightly open,
dead to the world. She was sleeping so deeply that
she did not notice what was happening to her husband.

Without warning, his eyes began to flicker and
move beneath his eyelids, as if he had slipped into
a massive rapid eye movement cycle. Then his
cracked, dried lips began to move.

"Spencer?" he whispered, his voice dry and
raspy. "Jesus Christ, Spencer . . ."

Natalie did not hear her husband, but the monitors began to come alive. The beeping became faster and more urgent as his heart rate accelerated
alarmingly. His respiration rate shot up and a sweat
broke on his brow. His eyes remained closed.

"What is *that*?" Streck's voice was full of alarm
and fear. "Spencer, do you *feel that*?"

The machines picked up the rising agitation and
began racing faster and faster.

"What is that? Oh God!" Streck thrashed as best
he could in the bed as if trying to run away from
his own nightmare. "Oh God, what is that? What's
happening?"

Suddenly, Alex Streck's eyes snapped open, but
they were unseeing, as if he thought himself in an-

other place. "Jesus!" He almost managed to yell this time. "What the hell is that?"

The monitors hit the red zone and an alarm split the air, the loud howl wakening Natalie instantly. She jumped to her feet and rushed to the bedside of her husband.

"Alex? Alex? What's wrong?"

The machinery kicked up another notch; a second alarm joined the first. Lights flickered and rolls of graph paper, scratched with a crazy quilt of ink, began to pour out of the mouth of one of the monitors.

"It hurts!" Alex wailed. "Oh God, it hurts!"

"*Alex*!" Natalie screamed. "*Wake up*!"

Somehow, Alex found enough breath in his weakened body to let out a terrible howl. "*Jesus! It hurts so much*!"

At that moment, the door flew open and a team of doctors and nurses swept into the room.

A nurse pounced on Natalie and tried to pull her away. "He's in pain," Natalie yelled. "He said something and he's in pain."

"Come with me, Mrs. Streck. Please . . ."

"He's dying!" wailed Natalie. "Save him."

"Let the doctors do their work," the nurse insisted, pulling her away from the bed.

"Oh, Alex!"

In the bed, Streck began to thrash wildly. A doctor and two more nurses fought to keep him down on the bed. Alex's eyes rolled back in his head and his body arched off the bed as if a million volts were running through every nerve, muscle, and synapse in his tortured body. Half-formed words broke from his spit-flecked lips as he struggled to say something, as if he was desperate to speak.

"Jesus, hold him," said one of the doctors, gritting his teeth. "Don't let him break out."

A nurse handed an enormous hypodermic needle to the doctor and without hesitation he jammed the horrific instrument into Streck's chest and jammed down the plunger, shooting the liquid deep into the astronaut's body.

The monitors were screaming—all except the one that measured Streck's heart rate. In a sickening monotone, the machine shut down and flatlined. Abruptly Alex stopped thrashing in the bed, his body falling flat and rigid.

"He's going," said one of the nurses matter-of-factly. "His vitals are dropping."

"Not yet, not yet," said the doctor firmly. "Get ready to defibrillate, nurse."

The nurse grabbed the portable defibrillator and pulled it to the side of the bed.

"Paddles," the doctor ordered. He grabbed the paddles and placed them against Streck's chest.

The nurse watched the machine. "Charging . . . Go!"

"Clear," the doctor ordered.

He gave the dying man an unholy blast of electricity right over the heart, Alex's body arched tight again but the heart rate remained at a sickening flat line.

"Still at zero," the nurse announced.

"Again!" yelled the doctor.

Another powerful charge of electricity surged through Alex Streck's body, convulsing him once again.

No one noticed that Jillian was watching this terrible tableau from the open door. Leaning heavily against his wife was Spencer. Jillian seemed horrified at what she was seeing. Spencer seemed curiously detached from the proceedings.

Another zap of electricity went through Alex— and as Alex's body spasmed he opened his eyes and looked directly at Spencer. Jillian saw it, the two men staring at one another and all the action in the room seemed to have stopped, the frantic sound in the room fading away. Spencer looked into Alex's eyes and nodded to him, a slight move of the head, as if he was saying "okay," giving Alex some kind of permission.

In that instant, motion and sound seemed to return to the room. Alex closed his eyes calmly and the heart monitor began to climb up from the flat line, working its way back to a weak but steady pace. The doctor and his nurses sighed.

"He's back," the doctor whispered. "We got him. It was close, but we got him back."

A moment or two later a nurse discovered Spencer and shooed him back to bed, clucking like a hen as she returned him to his room. Once Spencer had returned to his room a doctor entered, administered a sedative, and sent Spencer off to a very deep and dreamless sleep.

Then the doctor turned to Jillian. "There's nothing you can do here, Mrs. Armacost. He'll be out all night. Why don't you go home and get a good night's sleep . . ."

But there was no sleep for Jillian that night. She tossed and turned in her bed for a while, then threw aside the covers, pulled on a robe, and walked to the French doors and looked out into the still night. The sky was dappled with stars, white points of light that, on another night she would have found pretty and reassuring. Not tonight. Tonight they looked incomprehensible and tinged with evil.

5

After a couple of days of what doctors always called "observation," Spencer Armacost was released from the hospital, having been awarded a completely clean bill of health. In accordance with hospital policy, however, Spencer Armacost—clean bill of health and all—had to leave the facility not under his own steam but in a wheelchair. Jillian wheeled him to the front door and as the double doors swept open Spencer took a deep breath of the sweet, humid Florida air.

"That's good," he said.

"There's lots more out there," said Jillian smiling.

Spencer twisted his wheelchair seat and looked over his shoulder at his wife. He smiled broadly.

"You'll never guess what you missed, Jillian," he said. "A very big event."

"What did I miss?" she asked.

"The President called."

Jillian brought the wheelchair to an abrupt halt. "The President?" she asked.

"Of the United States of America," Spencer filled in, as if to distinguish him from other presidents. "He called this morning and told us that me and Alex were true American heroes. He wants us to go to Washington, D.C. so we can shake his hand in the Rose Garden. How do you like that? Being married to a true American hero."

"I love it," said Jillian simply.

"I figured."

"What did you say to the President?"

"Well," said Spencer, "I said that we would not have had a chance to be great American heroes if he and Congress hadn't cut our budget and forced us to put a piece of shit exploding satellite into orbit up there."

"You did not say that," said Jillian flatly. Although, knowing her husband as she did there was always the *possibility* that he had been less than respectful.

"But that's not all," Spencer continued.

"Really?"

Spencer nodded. "Then he said, as a way of showing his appreciation, he was going to send me a new car. A special new car, just for being a hero."

"How special?" Jillian asked, playing along now.

"The special kind that blows up when I put the key in the ignition," said Spencer deadpan.

Abruptly Jillian spun the wheelchair around until

they were face-to-face. "Spencer Armacost, did the President call you?"

Spencer nodded. "Yes, he did."

"And what did you say to him?"

Spencer opened his mouth to reply, but his wife cut him off, holding up her hand like a cop stopping traffic. "Ah-ah-ah," she cautioned. "Don't you lie to me."

"I wasn't going to lie . . . After he called me an American hero I said, 'Thank you very much, sir.' "

Jillian laughed leaned down and kissed him lightly, then turned the wheelchair back toward the door. "Now that's a little more like it," she said.

"Then I asked him what he was wearing and he hung up on me. Why do you think he did that? Can you imagine, me—an American hero and I get such disrespect."

"Amazing," said Jillian. "Some people just didn't learn good manners."

"My feelings exactly," said Spencer. He climbed out of the wheelchair and stretched. "I'll take it from here."

NASA had the ability to turn a public relations disaster into public relations gold. No sooner had Alex Streck and Spencer Armacost been released from the hospital, allowed a couple of days at home for a little rest and rehabilitation, then the press department of the agency called them back to the Cape for a space shuttle *Victory* victory celebration. It was a perfect opportunity for a carefully staged photo-op. And the icing on the cake was that the public had been invited.

Jillian Armacost and Natalie Streck sat with the wives of the astronauts on the mission on a bleacher erected on the lawn in front of the main administration building. Jammed in with them were dozens of tourists, curiosity seekers, and space buffs who ranged in age from eight to eighty.

The bleacher faced a huge American flag with the entire crew of the *Victory* posed in front of it. Over their heads flapping in the light breeze was a huge banner that read simply: WELCOME BACK!

A phalanx of photographers fired roll after roll of film at the seven astronauts, calling out to them by name to look this way and that. And to smile— above all to smile. The danger had passed, the program was back on track, and if you didn't believe it, here was photographic proof. The picture would appear around the world by that time tomorrow. The astronauts looked happy, the NASA officials looked happy. The spectators were delighted.

Only Natalie and Jillian looked concerned. They spoke in whispers, not daring to risk being overheard.

"Jill," Natalie asked. "Spencer . . . does he ever talk about it? About what happened?"

Jillian looked from the photo shoot and then back at the very worried-looking Natalie.

"How do you mean?" she asked warily, trying to stave off a series of painful questions. Questions she had asked herself since the day it all happened.

"I mean . . . does he ever say anything about

what it was like?'' Natalie hissed. "Did Spencer ever tell you what it was like? About what happened when they were alone up there?''

Jillian shook her head and touched Natalie's arm lightly. "It's okay, Natalie. They're back. Don't beat yourself up over it. Try to forget. Try to put it behind you.'' She spoke with a firm self-confidence she did not feel at all.

Natalie was not fooled by this show of certainty. She sensed that Jillian's brave face was nothing more than a mask, a façade. "He doesn't talk about it, does he?'' She did not wait for a response, feeling that she knew the answer already. "I know he doesn't talk about it,'' she went on. "Neither does Alex. Never. Not a word.''

Jillian nodded. "It must have been horrible,'' she said. "Why would they want to relive it?''

"How could they not?'' Natalie said, her voice rising slightly above her discreet whisper. "You're right, it must have been horrible. Those two minutes, they almost died, Jillian. I have thought of nothing else since it happened. So they must, too. It's only natural.''

"But they didn't die,'' Jillian protested. "They didn't die. They came back and they're well again.'' She looked over at the crew. All of them seemed genuinely happy. And why wouldn't they? Alex and Spencer had cheated death. It must be an exhilarating feeling. At least, it should be, shouldn't it?

Natalie could not leave it alone. The experience of the two men went around and around in her brain. "But they almost did, and to go through that, and never mention it. Never."

"Give them time, Natalie," said Jillian. "You have to give them time to understand what happened. It's not the sort of thing you can take in all at once, not something you can consume whole. It will take a long time for them to figure it all out. You have to believe that, Natalie. It makes sense, right?"

A look of pity came into Natalie's brown eyes. She had the feeling that Jillian was speaking from the heart—but for different reasons. "I know this must be hard for you, Jill."

"It's hard for everyone, Natalie."

"No," Natalie persisted, "hard for you in particular. I remember how bad it got for you after your parents died. It must have been horrible. Just like this is."

Natalie had crossed a line. Jillian's face turned cold and her words were clipped. She looked right at Natalie. "This has absolutely nothing to do with that," she said.

"It just scares me, Jillian," said Natalie, oblivious to the stab of pain she had jabbed into her friend. "It just scares me that he acts like it never happened."

Jillian looked from Natalie and then back to the photo shoot, which seemed to be coming to an end. Spencer and Alex were talking, their heads together as if they were whispering conspiratorially. Except for the cane that Alex Streck leaned against rather casually, neither men looked as if they had just survived a near miss with death in space followed by stays in the hospital. Spencer appeared to glow with health and Alex Streck seemed to have shed a few pounds and a few years, as if he had spent a week in a spa rather than having done excruciating time in a NASA intensive care unit.

As the photographers packed up their gear and the *Victory* crew dispersed, Jillian watched as two self-conscious kids edged into the scene. Both carried pictures of the *Victory* that the public relations guys had papered the visitors area with earlier that day. Spencer saw them looking longingly in his direction and he motioned to them, waving them over.

"Hey, kids," he said. "You two want an autograph or something like that?"

The two boys could not believe their luck. They raced over to the two astronauts. Spencer and Alex signed the pictures with a flourish and the two kids took off with their trophies. Jillian had seen the whole exchange and beamed with pride in her husband. Now *that* was Spencer Armacost—the real Spencer Armacost that she knew.

Jillian left Natalie and walked down the bleachers to her husband's side. He slid an arm around her slim waist and together they watched the kids run off.

"I know exactly what they're feeling," Spencer said. "They're going to grow up and be spacemen. I was going to do that. All my friends laughed when I told them . . ."

"But you did," said Jillian. "You showed them."

Spencer laughed a little. "Oh yeah . . . I sure showed them all right. I'm the envy of every adult in the country."

"You did what you set out to do," Jillian insisted. "You left your mark. That's more than some guy who works in a bank does. You became part of history. You did it . . ."

"I did it," he said quietly. "And now it's done." He looked at her and smiled. "All done."

Jillian returned his gaze but was also aware of Sherman Reese standing off to one side watching them. "What is done?" she asked. "What are you talking about."

"I'm resigning from the service," said Spencer bluntly. "That's what's done."

Jillian shook her head slightly, like a boxer shaking off a quick blow to the head. For a moment she was not entirely sure she had heard him correctly. She was completely taken aback by the announcement her husband had made in such a matter-of-fact manner.

"Is . . . is this because of what happened to you up there, Spencer?" Maybe Natalie was right after all, maybe something terrible had happened up there. Something that would alter his life—and by extension her own—forever.

Spencer took a deep breath and suddenly looked a little weary, as if he was not quite up to the task of explaining his reasons to her. "I'm done up there, Jillian," he said. "I'm finished with up there. I think I've just about had enough."

"What will you do?" she asked. She could not

imagine her husband doing anything but being involved in aviation.

Spencer smiled. "Believe it or not I got an offer, a job offer. Out of the blue, as it were."

"From who?" Jillian asked.

"An aerospace firm," Spencer answered. "It's an executive position. And it pays a lot of money, Jillian, bucketloads of money." Being an astronaut did not pay anything close to a single bucketload of money and there were a lot of things they had done without over the years. But neither of the Armacosts were particularly interested in getting a lot of money. It was usually the furthest thing from Spencer's mind.

"We don't care about money, Spencer," Jillian said. "We've always gotten by."

"Well, maybe we should start caring about it," he countered. "There's something to be said for having a savings account. Or so I'm told. I wouldn't know firsthand." He flashed her a smile. "Come on, Jill. Let's live a little."

"I have no objection to living a little, Spencer . . . But what do you know about being an executive? You are and always have been a flyer. I can't see you flying a desk."

"That's the beauty part," he said with another smile. "I don't have to actually be an executive . . . And as for flying a desk, after a few years that's exactly what I'll be doing around here. No one flies shuttle missions till the bitter end, you know."

"That's years off. Alex Streck didn't command his first mission till he was ten years older than you are now," said Jillian hotly. "You've got years of flying left in you."

"Sounds like you want me to go up there and take another crack at getting myself killed," he said. "I'm sure it could be arranged." He laughed when he said it, but she could sense that there was real hurt behind his words.

Jillian immediately felt like a complete heel and enfolded her husband in her arms. "You know that's not what I want. I want you to do what you want to do, Spencer . . . But why is this aerospace company hiring you? And why now?"

Spencer held her at arm's length and looked at her as if she was a little crazy. "I guess you don't read the papers, do you, dear? You are married to a true American hero. The President said so. So this company got to thinking that it might look nice to have the name of a true American hero on the letterhead."

"And you'd go for that? For bucketloads of money?" This did not sound like her husband at all.

"Beats working," he said with a grin. "Beats getting blown up in outer space . . ." The grin left his face. "There is something I have to tell you . . ."

"Oh boy," said Jillian. "I don't like the sound of this. Something nasty is headed this way."

"Nothing all that nasty," Spencer replied evenly. "Just New York City. The corporate headquarters . . . they're located up in New York City."

Now *that* really blindsided Jillian, a fact that took

her completely by surprise. "You're kidding!" she said. "You always said you hate New York City. What was it you always said: too many people living like that, it just isn't human."

Spencer sighed. "Things change. Now I want people. I want a lot of people. I wanted to be surrounded by people. Millions and millions of people."

Jillian could not believe what she was hearing. "But, Spencer, think about it," she protested. "We've made a life here, Spencer. Our friends are here, not to mention a job I love . . . everything. This was our life and we were happy with it until—"

Spencer looked away. He wasn't smiling or joking now. He raised his eyes to the sky. It wasn't a pretty blue Florida sky anymore, but had gone a milky white color.

Jillian knew what he was thinking about. Natalie was right. They did think about it. Those few minutes still haunted him and would for a long time to come.

"Tell me what it was like, Spencer," Jillian said gently. "Tell me about those two minutes . . . tell me . . ."

For a moment Spencer tried to speak, to put into the words the strange things that had happened to him, things that he himself did not understand. He had been unconscious so he had no idea what had transpired—he just knew that something had. And the words to describe it just would not come. Jillian could see the pain and distress on the face of her husband and she moved quickly to soothe away the hurt and the terror of the recent past.

"I'm sorry, Spence . . :" she whispered. "I'm so sorry. Don't think about it, okay?"

Spencer turned her face to his and kissed her warmly and deeply. She felt herself going limp in his arms, holding him close, not wanting to let him go for anything.

Spencer spoke over her shoulder. "I know what I'm asking, Jill. I know how hard it will be for you. I know what this place means to you. I know what these people mean to you, too. I . . . I just don't think I can be here anymore. Can you do it? Can you come away with me and do this thing in New York? If it doesn't work out, we will have tried and we can move on to something else . . . I promise we won't be caught—trapped—there. But I think I have to try it."

Jillian pulled away and looked at her husband, tears in her eyes. "You came and took me away once, when I needed it," she said softly. "I've always wanted to do the same for you." She nodded decisively. "Let's go to New York."

"And be surrounded by people?"

Jillian nodded again. "And be surrounded by people."

"Love me?" Spencer asked.

"Forever," Jillian replied.

"Really?" said Spencer slyly, coyly, a grin on his face. "How come you love me?"

"Because you're cute," said Jillian.

"How cute?" Spencer demanded.

"Don't push it," Jillian replied, a touch of iron in her soft voice.

"As cute as a spaghetti-eatin' dog?" he asked.

Both of them were so engrossed in their little game that neither of them noticed that Sherman Reese was watching them intently. And Reese was watching them so closely that he did not notice that Alex Streck was staring at Sherman Reese.

"Cute as a spaghetti-eating dog?" said Jillian laughing. "Let me think it over."

"Come on, Jilly," said Spencer. "Ain't nothing cuter than a spaghetti-eatin' dog . . ."

6

"Are you going to live in space?"

"No, Paula, we won't be going to live in space."
Virtually every student in Jillian's second grade
class had asked her a similar question since the beginning of the goodbye party. No one looked like
they were having a very good time, despite the tray
of cupcakes and the brightly colored balloons an-
chored to chairs and table legs.

It was difficult for a bunch of kinds to lose a
popular teacher in the middle of the year, and Jillian
felt a certain amount of guilt for dropping such a
bombshell on them. But she also knew that kids
were resilient and that not too many weeks would
pass before they had adapted to a new and probably
beloved teacher. Mrs. Armacost would be nothing
more than a dim, if pleasant, memory.

It turned out that Paula had a follow-up question.
She wanted more information on this troubling subject. "But your husband lives in space," she lisped,
"and he's taking you back with him, so aren't you

going to go and live in space?'' It made perfect sense to her seven-year-old way of looking at things.

"My husband *used* to work in space," Jillian explained patiently. "Now he and I are going to go live in a place called New York City. That's up north."

"Oh." The little girl took this in, thinking about it for a moment. Then she asked, "Mrs. Armacost?"

"Yes, Paula?"

"When your husband is in space, does he ever see God up there?" she asked matter-of-factly.

It was, Jillian thought, a damn good question, but before she could answer, a little boy named Calvin ran up to her.

"What about aliens? Does he see aliens?" The words tumbled out of the boy's wide red mouth. "Does your husband bring a laser gun in case there are aliens? If I were going into space and I saw aliens I'd make sure I brought two laser guns. A little one for my pocket and then a big laser rifle. Does your husband have a laser rifle? Does he bring it home from work with him? Does it work here on Earth or does it only work in space? Mrs. Armacost, does it?"

Calvin was panting now, as if he had just run up a couple of flights of steep stairs.

Jillian laughed. "You know what, Calvin?"

"What, Mrs. Armacost?"

"I'm going to miss you." She looked around at the kids frolicking in the classroom and felt a lump in her throat. She knew she was going to miss all of them.

The "grown up" farewell party for Jillian and Spencer Armacost was childish in its own way, a childishness brought on largely by the consumption of copious amounts of alcohol.

The party was being held in a tent behind a NASA watering hole called Jack's Tavern and by the time the party really got going, the tent was packed. There were the men with short hair who had worn crew cuts since the fifties and saw no reason for a change, there were healthy, middle-aged women in Bermuda shorts whose skin suggested that they spent more time than they should in the Florida sun. There was a gaggle of NASA geeks with black-rimmed eyeglasses and a pallor that suggested they did not spend enough time out of doors. Nan was there, making eyes at the bartender, but he didn't have much time for her—he was working hard to slake the thirsts of the merrymakers. Parked on a table near the bar was a sheet cake shaped like a space shuttle with "Farewell Spence and Jill" unsteadily embroidered in frosting across the midships.

The entire crew of the *Victory* was there as well as Sherman Reese and the Director himself. Not even the appearance of the big bosses could dampen the high spirits of the party.

Someone was trying to make a speech through a blizzard of static and feedback. "They asked me to write a speech. A farewell for you, Commander—''

There were interruptions from the audience, cries of ''No!'' and ''Don't go!''

But the man persisted, determined to give his speech. ''But I'm a mission specialist and that specialty does not include speech giving. I tried to tell ya—''

A man called Tom Sullivan, one of the crew of the *Victory*, stepped out of the crowd. ''You are absolutely right, Stan. You can't give a speech. I will.''

To general applause Stan relinquished the microphone and Sullivan stepped up. He grinned drunkenly at the crowd.

''Spence,'' he said, ''you have been our commander lo these many years . . .''

''*Lo these many years . . .*'' the crowd roared back. Farewell speeches tended to follow a standard script.

''We figured that there must be some way to tell you how we truly feel . . .''

Jillian had been having a pretty good time, though she had been to plenty of farewell bashes just like this one, and was doing her best to get into the spirit of the thing until she looked through the crowd and saw Alex and Natalie Streck. In contrast to the general good humor that pervaded the gathering, the Strecks were not having a good time. In fact, though their words were drowned out by revelry, the Strecks were in the middle of a very nasty argument.

Alex was reaching for a plastic glass filled almost to the brim with a clear liquid—a very stiff gin or vodka, maybe—and she saw Natalie try to stop him from taking it. A flash of anger crossed his face as he snatched at the drink, grabbing it so forcefully that a good deal of the liquid slopped over the brim, raising another furious look from Alex. No one else had seen the action and if the Strecks cared about being observed they were doing nothing to hide themselves. Most eyes were on the stage where Tom Sullivan had been joined by two more members of the crew of the *Victory*, Shelly Carter and Pat Elliot. The three of them were joined shoulder over shoulder and swaying to a music that only they seemed to be able to hear. It was plain that the three of them were going to sing whether the crowd wanted them to or not.

"Commander," Tom Sullivan slurred into the microphone, "this one's for you." He looked over his shoulder at the bartender. "Maestro, if you please . . ."

The bartender hit something on a karaoke machine and the night was flooded with an extremely loud set of opening chords for "My Way." The difference was, this wasn't the "My Way" that had become the anthem of Frank Sinatra. This was the mocking, sarcastic, and rather funny version of the same song as performed by the late Sid Vicious. While it is widely held that astronauts and NASA types are generally square, the Sex Pistols had managed to penetrate to this part of the space program twenty years after their heyday.

As the intro for the song kicked into high gear, Jillian saw Alex Streck raise the glass to his lips and drink it down as if it contained nothing more powerful than a soft drink. Then she remembered: *vodka* ... Vodka was Alex Streck's beverage of choice. From across the room she winced as she seemed to feel the heavy belt of alcohol that Alex had just smacked himself with. Natalie too looked away in pain. In that moment she hated her husband. And in that moment she hated to see him hurt himself like that.

The three drunken astronauts burst into song, singing every bit as badly as the dead punk rocker they were trying to emulate. The crowd screamed and laughed at the singing, and everyone was enjoying the parody—even Spencer was enjoying the antics of the singers on the stage—everyone, that is, except Alex and Natalie. The entire audience pointed at Spencer for the last line about doing it "his" way.

There were hoots and hollers from the crowd as Spencer took a bow. As he did the guitar began to crank and almost simultaneously the crowd began to dance. The music was harsh and driving now, assaulting the dancers and listeners, as if somehow the lyrics had drained a portion of the goodwill from the party. Everyone seemed lit up with the rock and roll and the flowing booze. The under-twenty-five crowd started slam dancing, throwing themselves against each other in bone-crunching smashes, as if they didn't care who got hurt. The older types were at the bar throwing down beers and hard liquor as if it were their last night on earth. The music pulsed so loud it seemed to split the darkness and wash away any rational thought or action.

Jillian caught sight of Spencer, his hair awry, laughing as he was drawn into the frenzy, caught up in the mass of gyrating bodies packed together on what passed for a dance floor. It was strange to see one of the NASA geeks stage diving from the bar into the throng, his black tie flapping, the pens from his breast pocket scattering. He hit the solid mass of bodies, then disappeared from view.

Jillian was crouched in a corner, as if protecting herself from her own farewell party, but she could see what was going on, as if through an old kinescope. As legs jerked and arms waved she could make out the action in shaky sequence. Then, through the wild antics of the dancers she saw Alex Streck again. He was taking the glass from his lips and staring as a red bloom appeared in the middle of his vodka, a large gout of his own blood. His nose was bleeding, the gore dripping straight into the glass of colorless liquid.

Jillian jumped to her feet and tried to move through the crowd toward him. Sweaty bodies, damp and clammy and as immovable as sandbags, stood in her way.

The singers screamed till ears hurt.

Jillian never lost sight of Alex. He was just standing there, dumbly, as if attempting to figure out how his own blood could be flowing from his body. His face was stained red with blood from his brow to his chin but he did not seem to be in any pain. No one else had seen this except Natalie and Jillian. Natalie was yelling something in her husband's ear—not words of anger this time, but urgent words of interrogation. Jillian could not hear the questions but she could imagine what she was saying, the kind of thing a doctor or a nurse might ask: *How much have you had to drink, do you feel dizzy, nauseous, do you remember a blow to the head . . . ?*

Alex staggered a bit and Natalie threw her arms around his waist to hold him up, but he was too heavy for her. Suddenly he spasmed as if shot and pitched straight forward, headfirst, landing on a table covered with glasses and beer bottles. His weight brought the whole thing down, glass and plastic shattering under him.

Natalie screamed and Jillian ran for her. But still the music and the frenzy of the crowd overpowered the sickening sound of a man falling, a woman screaming.

Natalie sucked in another lungful of air and screamed again and this time her plaintive wail cut through the noise. It cut through the music and the laughter and the drunkenness. That unholy scream cut the cacophony, slicing it off, as if decapitating it. The music stopped. The dancing stopped.

There was nothing but stillness in that party except a screaming woman and the red blood pumping from the nose of a bleeding man.

All eyes were on Alex. He lay on the concrete floor, the broken glass and plastic spread under him like a painful carpet. Alex twisted and writhed on the beer-soaked stone, his body going thorough a horrible sequence of paroxysms, muscle-wrenching contortions that looked from second to second as if his own body would tear itself apart. Not one sober person in that crowd—and there weren't many—gave him too much longer to live.

The singing and dancing stopped. Karaoke continued to blast out of the speaker until the bartender got the brainstorm to stop it. Suddenly all was silence there in that tent behind a Florida honky tonk—silent save for the wailing of Natalie and the ghastly beating of Alex's fists against the concrete floor. His clenched hands smashed into the hard floor, into the shattered glass. His hands were flayed, his fingers split, and his blood gushed.

No one tried to save him until Spencer acted. He broke through the crowd and dropped like a wrestler down on to Streck's body, slamming him against the cement floor, grabbing his bloody hands and pinning them as if scoring a point. Blood spurted from a dozen wounds, from Streck's nose, from his hands, from his torn cheek, the hot fresh blood spraying Spencer as if from a hose, soaking him.

It was as if Alex Streck was determined to bleed to death. He fought the help that had come to his aid. He battled against Alex, and Tom Sullivan (who had stopped singing and dropped down on Streck's chest), and he fought against his wife who tried to hold his thrashing legs. Alex threw Natalie off him like a bronco bucking a green cowboy.

His real adversary was Spencer. He had Streck's blood-slick hands clasped in his own and he was shouting something to the older man, looking into his eyes as if telegraphing a message that only the two of them could understand.

Then, without warning, Spencer lowered his mouth to Alex's and began administering CPR, breathing for his mission commander, pinching off the nose of the older man and trying to push his own breath into his lungs. Spencer looked into Alex's eyes as they were locked mouth-to-mouth and Spencer shook his head from side to side.

"No," he was saying. "No, no, no, no . . ."

But Alex had ceased to understand. He summoned up the strength for one more deep, gut-wrenching muscular spasm and he convulsed, throwing Alex and the others from his body. His blood-filled mouth pulled away from Alex's lips and he screamed, yelling his lungs out in pain and anguish—a sound louder than the howls of his tormented wife, a scream that screamed all the life out his body.

When the shriek finally died away, Alex Streck fell back on the beer-covered concrete behind that shitty bar in Florida . . . and he was dead. It was as if he had chosen to screech the very life out of his soul.

Before anyone else could react, Natalie dropped to her knees next to her husband, the fabric of her blue jeans soaking up the thick black blood that had flowed out of his body. She knew he was dead and she picked up his heavy head and cradled it in her own strong arms, as if it was a sacred relic. She laid her tear-streaked face on his blood-encrusted face and whimpered, "No, no, no, no . . . oh, Alex, please, no . . ." The tears ran from her eyes and cut pale courses through the blood on his cheeks like rivers.

Everything was so quiet, and so suddenly. The merrymakers, the party-goers, the hangers-on suddenly felt as if they had intruded at something sacred.

The night had become as quiet as the grave.

Quiet but for the grieving of a woman lost. "Oh," she said, "Alex . . . oh . . . Oh, my Alex, what did they do to you?"

Natalie Streck, the lifeless body of her beloved husband clutched in her arms, looked up at the assembled crowd. The astronauts, the NASA geeks, the Mission Control guys, the crew of the *Victory* . . . she looked at Spencer and Jillian Armacost. Sherman Reese was still there but the Director was nowhere to be seen.

"What happened?" she asked quietly. "What happened to my husband?"

In the distance insistent sirens could be heard. They were drawing nearer with the passing of every second.

Natalie still wept, but she knew what she wanted to say. "What's going to happen to us all?"

In the days that followed, those who had been at the farewell party for Spencer and Jillian Armacost would speculate a great deal about the events of that evening and the words that Natalie Streck had spoken that night. The general consensus was that Alex Streck's injuries in space had been underestimated by the doctors back on earth and that he had been given a clean bill of health well before he deserved one. The injury, the excitement and yes, even the excessive drinking had contributed to his huge coronary that night.

And whatever Natalie had to say was a result of nothing more than stress and hysteria—after all, the only thing you had to hear about was what had come next.

And besides, look at Spencer Armacost, they said. He sailed through this with flying colors. He and Alex had been through the same ordeal, the only difference was Spencer was a whole lot younger than Alex—and those years made all the difference.

The wags around NASA gave each other slight, knowing looks and winked and said, "See, you leave the agency, you head up north, or out west or to the coast if Boeing is interested in you, and then you make yourself something like a ton of money. You cash in the way Spencer and Jill did. Who could blame you? It was the lifers like Alex Streck and that nutty wife of his . . . they were the ones you had to worry about . . ."

They talked about it endlessly—at lunch, or during their morning commutes, at dinner, and in bed with their wives. Do your time at NASA, do what you love for as long as you can . . . Then, and only then, it's time for a change. You will have served your country. You will have served science. But there comes a time when you have to serve yourself. Any damn fool could see that was the wise thing to do. The trouble was Alex Streck hadn't seen it that way and neither had Natalie. And that was their downfall.

Now Spencer Armacost and his wife Jillian— they knew how the game was played and they got out when it was time to. Get the hell out while you're still sane and can make some serious money. I mean, look at Spencer and Jill, did they play it right or what? I think I'll give Spencer a call myself when I think it's time to bail.

He'd never let down a friend. Not a friend from the old days . . .

7

The Director himself stood at the podium in the press room. He shuffled some papers for a moment then leaned into the microphone to speak to the assembled crowd of press people. His voice was deep and solemn.

"I have a very brief prepared statement and then there will be time for some prepared questions."

Sherman Reese stood behind the Director scanning the faces of the cadre of reporters.

The Director got right to the point. "Captain Alex Streck died last night at 8:55." He paused a moment to let the words sink in. Most of the reporters in the room worked the science beat or were local Florida reporters. Most of them were on first-name terms with many of the astronauts. The loss of just one of them was like a death in a tight-knit family.

The Director continued. "The cause of death has been determined to have been a massive stroke. Something that the surgeons are calling a severe insult to the brain. As many of you know, Alex was an asset to this program in ways well beyond his professional expertise. There is no doubt that his loss is a setback for the program itself and an agonizing loss for those of us who knew him and valued him as a friend. There will be a private ceremony—''

Sherman Reese was surprised to see tears well in the Director's eyes and hear his voice falter. He had never imagined that his boss would be an emotional man.

An eager reporter took advantage of the pause and pounced with a question. ''Was Captain Streck's stroke brought on by an injury he sustained in space during the last mission of the space shuttle *Victory*?'' he asked.

The Director seemed to welcome the fact that he could get off the hot seat with some grace.

''I don't know. I'll let Dr. Conlin answer. Doctor?'' he said, gesturing toward a man in his fifties. ''Would you come up here please?''

Dr. Conlin stepped to the podium microphone. ''The, uh, post mortem had determined that Captain Streck had an undiagnosable congenital predisposition for stroke,'' he said, looking grave. His glasses flashed in the bright television flood lights. ''We had no way of knowing that the micro arteries in his brain were weak to begin with. It is a condition almost impossible to detect until there is problem with the patient . . .''

In the moment of hesitation all of the reporters shouted a dozen variations on the same question.

"What about the injury on the *Victory?* Did that kill him?"

Dr. Conlin nodded. "The injury he sustained outside the space shuttle caused an onset of undetectable bleeding which led to his death by cerebrovascular accident."

"That a stroke?" someone shouted.

"That is correct," said the Doctor.

"Is Commander Armacost in any danger?" someone shouted from the crowd.

It was a surprise to hear Spencer's name mentioned on TV. Both Jillian and Spencer stopped what they were doing and looked at the television set. Both were getting ready to go to Alex Streck's memorial and were listening to the televised news conference as they got dressed. Jillian was well ahead of her husband. She was wearing a black two-piece linen suit, a skirt topped by a short double-breasted jacket. There was a simple strand of pearls at her throat.

Spencer, by contrast, had just stepped out of the shower, was wearing a terrycloth bathrobe and was facing the mirror in the bathroom. Both taps ran in the sink but they could hear the TV over the sound of the rushing water.

"Commander Armacost has been through an intensive array of examinations and tests," Dr. Conklin answered. "It is the opinion of myself and my colleagues that the commander is no more danger than any one of us."

"Couldn't you have said the same thing about

Captain Streck?'' yelled one of the journalists. "After all, he underwent a series of tests after the explosion in space, too. Maybe you could have missed something in him, too."

Spencer looked into the mirror and caught the eye of his wife standing behind him. "Seems like they've got me dead and buried already," he said with a crooked grin.

"The press loves a story. Particularly if it's got a nice juicy dead body in it . . ." She put her hands on his shoulders. "I'm sure you are just fine, Spencer."

"Sure I am," he said. He picked up his razor and examined his beard in the mirror.

On the television set Dr. Conlin was assuring everyone that, indeed, Commander Armacost was in fine fettle. "Commander Armacost is considerably younger than Captain Streck," the doctor explained. "And had no predisposition to stroke, as far as we can determine. There's no family history, no history of sustained elevated blood pressure, no blood gas irregularities . . ."

Spencer seemed to have lost all interest in having his health discussed on live national television. Instead, he swathed his face in shaving cream. Then he picked up his razor and looked at it as if seeing it for the first time and was not quite sure how he was supposed to use the thing. Slowly and tentatively he raised the blade to his skin, hesitated a moment, then drew the blade across his chin. Instantly a minute line of blood appeared in the froth of the shaving cream.

Jillian saw him do it and she went to him and took the hand that held the razor in her hand and examined it closely. Blood dripped from the blade.

"Spencer . . ." Her voice was full of concern. "You've cut yourself, honey."

"I'm okay," Spencer said. "Really, it's nothing. The television just threw me off a little. That's all."

"Let me do it, Spencer," said Jillian. She tried to take the razor from his hand.

"I'm okay, Jillian," Spencer insisted. "Please, just leave it alone. I can handle it."

With her free hand she dabbed at the blood on his chin with a piece if tissue paper. Then she looked into her husband's eyes, a quizzical smile on her face. "I think I see the problem here . . . Spencer, you are right-handed," she said.

They both looked at the razor. Spencer was holding the blade in his left hand.

Jillian took it from him. "Let me," she said very softly, as if she was talking to a child. "It's okay, let me do it, honey. Please . . ." And slowly, Spencer opened his left hand and allowed Jillian to take the razor. Slowly, gently, as if dealing with a spooked horse, she raised the blade to his neck and ran it over his skin.

Spencer's eyes looked sad and closed to the world around him. "Alex is dead," he whispered. Suddenly he looked like a little boy who had lost his best friend. Bereft and lost, foundering at sea in a ocean of melancholy emotions.

Jillian knew that look and was just as heartbroken for her husband. "I know," she said. There were tears welling in her eyes now. "I know, Spencer . . ."

She looked at her husband in the mirror, but he looked past her, staring into at his own reflection, gazing into his own eyes as if looking into the workings of his own mind.

Jillian and Spencer had never thought that the Strecks were particularly observant Jews, but Natalie was insistent that the instant she returned from the cemetery where Alex had been buried the seven days of shiva had to begin. The week of mourning was intense and the rituals had been followed to the letter. Natalie had covered all the mirrors, drawn the drapes to darken the entire house and had served the "seudat havrach" meal to the members of the immediate family.

By the time Jillian and Spencer arrived the Strecks' relatives had been joined by a number of men and women from the NASA program, as well as other friends and neighbors. Men and women clad in funereal black stood around the Streck room feeling self-conscious and talking in hushed tones.

Periodically the front door opened, admitting along with guests harsh shafts of bright afternoon sunlight. Spencer and Jillian entered on a blade of light, shutting the door quickly to restore the crepuscular gloom of the room. Nan threaded her way through the crowd and hugged Jillian tight and long.

"You okay?" Nan asked.

Jillian nodded. "Yeah. It's hard, but we'll be okay. It's hard to believe he's gone."

Spencer pointed to a small clutch of NASA people standing in a corner. "I'll be over there," Spencer whispered and made his way across the room.

"Where's Natalie?" Jillian asked Nan.

"Upstairs," Nan replied. "She's been asking for you. She wanted to make sure you were here before they said Kaddish."

Jillian nodded and walked toward the staircase. As she climbed the steps she looked down on the crowd of mourners. Her husband was already talking to a knot of NASA tech types and did not see her. She noticed that Sherman Reese was looking up at her as she climbed. She assumed that the Director must be around there someplace. One did not travel without the other.

The door to Natalie's bedroom was half open and Jillian pushed it aside. It was gloomy within, but Jillian could make out Natalie, prone on the bed. She was dressed in her black dress and even still had her black high heels on her feet.

"Natalie?" Jillian spoke into the shadows.

"Jillian?" She slurred the single word. Jillian took a step closer and saw an open vial of sedatives on the bedside table. It was only natural that she take something. She sat down on the edge of the bed and brushed a loose strand of hair from Natalie's eyes.

"How are you holding up?" Jillian asked. "I know it's going to be hard . . ."

Natalie did not answer Jillian's questions, not directly anyway. "They talked to him, Jillian. They talked to him all the time. They talked to him every night."

Jillian touched Natalie's cheek and gently wiped away a tear. She said nothing, knowing it was better to let Natalie speak even if little or nothing she said made any sense.

"I couldn't understand them," Natalie continued. Her eyes were fixed on some point far off in the distance, some place beyond the confines of that gloomy bedroom. "I couldn't understand them, Jill, not while Alex was alive. I couldn't . . . but now I do."

"Who talked to him, Natalie?" Jillian asked quietly. "Who talked to Alex?"

Natalie's eyes closed as the drugs and the exhaustion kicked in. "Who talked to him?" she murmured. "They did, Jillian. They did. They talked all the time . . ."

Suddenly Jillian felt terribly afraid and she shivered as if a chill had just come over her. "Who are they, Natalie?" she asked urgently. "Tell me who they are."

Natalie said nothing. But as she slipped into her drug-induced sleep she pointed at something on the far side of the room. Jillian followed the direction and saw that Natalie was pointing at a simple, cheap radio. Jillian looked from the radio and then back to the slumbering Natalie.

"Natalie?" Jillian asked.

But she was out cold. Jillian looked back to the radio and then began to walk from the room. Then,

very distinctly, she heard Natalie's voice out loud:
"It's not a dream, Jillian."

She turned but Natalie's eyes remained closed,
her chest rose and fell and she had not stirred.

Jill came back downstairs and poured herself a glass
of water and watched her husband.

Spencer was engaged in an odd, rather guarded
conversation with Sherman Reese, a discussion that
was wholly out of place in a bereaved household.
Reese had not wanted to bring it up at all, not while
shiva was being sat for Alex Streck, but with the
Armacosts' imminent departure he took a chance
and expressed his fears to Spencer there and then
and the hell with the consequences.

Spencer had not been happy to be approached
like this, and he had a hard time getting a handle
on exactly what it was that Reese was getting at. It
seemed to involve further medical exams—in
search of God knows what—even though Spencer
had been officially separated from NASA and hon-
orably discharged from the armed forces.

"I assure you," Reese was saying, "this will
hardly take a moment of your time, Commander,
and it could be quite important. For the future of
the program and the agency." Reese knew there
was no better way to get an old astronaut to co-
operate than to run the old space program flag up
the mast.

But it did not work with Spencer Armacost. At
least, not this time, anyway.

"I appreciate your concern, Mr. Reese," said

Spencer evenly, "but I have been poked with more than enough needles to last me a lifetime, you understand. And your superiors have given me a clean bill of health. That's good enough for me."

Reese nodded vigorously. "I know they have, Commander. I know they have. It's probably nothing at all, but I think it would make sense to have—"

Spencer's eyes narrowed and he looked at Reese with a certain amount of suspicion. "Tell me, do your bosses know that you want to do this? Does the Director know? Or is this a purely extra curricular activity on your part, Mr. Reese?"

Reese looked at the floor and shook his head slowly. "No one knows about this. No one but me. And now you, of course." He looked up and directly into Spencer's eyes. "And I'm sure I can count on your discretion in this matter, can't I?"

"Of course," said Spencer with a thin smile.

As he spoke the lights in the house blinked off and then after a second or two blinked on again. There was a loud, fast zapping noise and the acrid smell of smoke from an electrical fire.

"Fuse?" someone wondered aloud. There were a couple of seconds of silence, which was immediately dispelled by the loud, high-pitched sound of a little girl screaming. She was upstairs.

Jill dropped the glass in her hand and dashed for the stairs. The screaming was coming from the bathroom at the end of the hall. She pushed open the door and saw a little girl—maybe eight or nine years old—standing in the doorway. She was frozen in place by fear, staring at something horrible at the far end of the bathroom.

Natalie Streck was standing in front of the sink, both faucets gushing water into an overflowing basin, water splashing to the tile floor. Both of Natalie's hands were in the sink, her hands wrapped like claws around the cheap radio, the one from her bedroom. The radio that she said had spoken incessantly to her dead husband. It was as if she was trying to drown the thing.

A power cord led from an electrical outlet into the sink. Natalie's body was trembling, her hair on end, a crackle and fizzle at the corners of her mouth, her eyes wide. Natalie was dead, electrocuted by the radio that she said had killed her husband.

Almost in a trance, Jillian took a step closer to the horrible sight. The little girl continued to scream. But Jillian heard her name loud and clear over the shrieking of the child.

"Jillian! Look out!" Spencer grabbed her and pulled her back from the pool of electrified water in the middle of the bathroom floor. She had almost stepped in it and joined her friend in a horrible death. It had been so close and she had not even realized it.

Natalie still stood, her dead eyes staring into the mirror. The little girl continued to scream. Jillian gaped at the scene. It would be a long time before she forgot those eyes and the sound of that scream.

8

Jillian Armacost had had her doubts about Spencer leaving NASA and the two of them leaving Florida, particularly for a destination like New York City. But with the deaths of Alex and Natalie Streck, each grotesque in its own, unique way, she knew she could not stay there any longer. The place was haunted for her now, and perhaps a radical change of place and style of living might be enough to banish the bad memories and the hellish images.

And yet New York was quite a stretch. There were two fundamental problems to deal with. First off, the city itself—the noise, the confusion, the polyglot population—was disconcerting at first, but Jillian was sure that she could adapt to it.

With the other problem she wasn't so sure. Suddenly and without warning, she found that she was rich. The aerospace corporation that had hired Spencer was paying him in a year what NASA paid in a decade. In addition to the salary, the company provided a vast duplex company apartment in the heart of the Upper East Side, along with a company car—a Jaguar—that came with a private parking space that cost as much as the rent for a two-bedroom apartment back in Florida. Jillian just wasn't used to being able to afford anything she happened to see and the effects were quite disconcerting.

Oddly enough, and to Jillian's immense surprise, Spencer took to the New York way of living without the slightest hesitation. Without a second thought all of his old clothes went to Goodwill and he spent a couple of days outfitting himself at Bergdorf's, Paul Stuart, and Barney's. Jillian had to admit that her husband looked pretty sharp and well turned out in his new clothes, but somehow he did not *quite* look like Spencer—that is, *Jillian's* Spencer.

In addition to all this, Jillian was not quite used to the social life that went along with corporate life. It seemed as if they went out at least five nights out of seven, but always during the week, never on Saturdays or Sundays—rich New Yorkers appeared to vanish on weekends—which was quite a bit more socializing than Jillian was used to.

The nature of the entertainment was different, too. Until the move to New York, Spencer and Jillian had socialized in bars not unlike the one where their tragic farewell party had been held—back-country taverns where the drink of choice was long-necked beers, where people only had scotch on their birthdays.

Now they went out to dinner almost every night.

New Yorkers of a certain type made a fetish out of
first-class restaurants and if you didn't know someone on the inside of the most chic restaurants in the
city, you might have to wait up to a month for a
reservation. Jillian had to admit the restaurants were
fabulous, beautifully designed, with exquisite food
faultlessly served. One thing puzzled her about
these palatial places—she wondered how they
could charge such extortionate prices for such minute portions. But since they moved to New York,
price had ceased to be a consideration. The company credit card paid for all—Spencer's expense
account was virtually without limit. And, Jillian noticed, he seemed to enjoy using it.

Dinner was almost always preceded by a cocktail
party. Sometimes they were held in fabulous apartments with million-dollar views of Central Park,
sometimes they were held in places not normally
open for parties like the Temple of Dendur at the
Metropolitan Museum of Art or at the sculpture garden of the Museum of Modern Art. But wherever
they might be held they always had one thing in
common. When Spencer announced that they had
to go to yet another cocktail party and Jillian
groaned and moaned about it he could always silence her with a single reason. So far, it had never
failed.

"We have to go," he said. "It's business."

That night, "business" took them to a party in the
gargantuan lobby of a building on Wall Street that
had been built as the old U.S. Customs House for

the Port of New York. But these days Fifty-five Wall Street housed a bank—a bank very interested in doing business with the company that featured Spencer's name so prominently on its stationery.

For once Jillian did not object to going out to a cocktail party—Spencer had told her that there was a rumor that the big boss, the head of the company might attend this particular function. She had heard so much about the mysterious Jackson McLaren that she was very anxious to meet him—even if it meant another night out on the social scene.

Fifty-five Wall Street had been built by the same firm of architects that designed Grand Central Station and some of the pharoanic scale of that building lingered in this one. The lobby was vast, a space so huge and beautiful it was almost daunting. The ceiling seemed so high above the pavement it appeared to have been lost in the night sky. Fifty-five Wall, the high cathedral of high finance, was built to prove that money was the greatest power known to man.

The power of the room and the people in it had the usual effect on Jillian. She felt absolutely insignificant. She stood with a glass of champagne in her hand watching men and women in faultless dinner jackets move through the crowd bearing trays of canapés almost too beautiful to be eaten.

Jillian surveyed the crowd. She was becoming familiar with the New York types. There were the old men, men in their seventies and eighties, men so rich they were worth more than some small countries. They had been so rich for so long that they automatically commanded a certain kind of respect. Accordingly, they were treated like heads of state. These men were usually attended by women of the same age, perhaps a year or two younger, but never more. These were first wives who had married these men fifty or more years before, members of a generation who believed that a marriage vow was something that was not to be taken lightly—particularly the "for richer or poorer" part.

Beneath these wealthy old lions were the men in their fifties and sixties, men who still had careers as CEOs and CFOs or in brokerage firms and banks. These men almost all had one thing in common—they had started out in their banks or brokerages back in the late fifties and early sixties, grateful to have a job with a nice firm and hoping to have something approaching a lengthy and comfortable career. They married their high school, college, or hometown sweethearts and bought little houses in the suburbs on Long Island, in Westchester, and in New Jersey. They never missed the 5: 23 train home because back in those simpler days there was nothing to be gained working late, tracking something as bizarre as a foreign stock market or the track record of a company manufacturing something in another country—like Japanese cars, for example.

The idea was to take the train into work in the morning, do your job, have a couple of drinks at lunch, go back to work, leave your desk at five on the dot to make your train back to Islip or Scarsdale or Ridgewood and hearth and home. The closest they got to a New York experience was having a Manhattan at lunch. One thing these guys in their short-sleeve shirts and crew cuts and Brook Brothers suits had never figured on happening was getting rich. They hoped they would make it up to twenty-five or thirty thousand bucks by the time they were in their forties, but real money—that was an impossibility. Bankers and brokers didn't get rich. They made *other* people rich.

Then everything changed. The market exploded. Investment banking started to pay well and the wage slaves started to get rich. Moderately rich at first—they bought nice jewelry for their wives, their kids didn't have to apply for financial aid when they went to college. And Dad got rid of his Dodge and bought himself a boat or maybe a sports car—an MG, perhaps or maybe a Thunderbird or a Corvette. No one knew it at the time but those shiny new sports cars were the beginning of the end, the thin edge of the wedge.

Then everything changed again. These guys were too old for the summer of love or the Vietnam war, but they felt that something fresh was in the air— and that was the bull market of the sixties that erupted like a skyrocket and yanked the wage earners into higher levels of wealth, heights they had never expected to attain.

And *that's* when everything *really* changed. Miraculously, stock brokering and investment banking came to be considered *sexy* occupations and suddenly, the wage earners were no kidding, honest-

to-God rich. They felt like they could do anything—
and they did anything they chose. The first wife,
the college sweetheart, the hometown girl was the
first thing to go. Resentful kids suddenly had step-
mothers who were younger than they were and bitter first wives took healthy alimony payments and
opened gift shops that failed after a year or two.

The men were now in their fifties and sixties and
had beautiful young wives in their twenties. The
first wives got the house in Scarsdale, because their
divorced husbands were now living in Manhattan,
because that was the only place that the new, trophy
wife would consider living. And it had to be on
Central Park West, or the Upper East Side, and definitely *west* of Third. The apartments were huge by
New York standards, but rarely the size of their old
garage out in suburbia. And they had to have a
playroom and a room for the nanny, because these
rich men in their sixties now had a second set of
children in diapers—children these men would not
live long enough to see drive a car.

But right now, they were the most powerful men
on Wall Street, which meant that they were some
of the most powerful people on the face of the
earth.

Beneath them were the wannabes. The class of
wage earners was gone forever, replaced by the
overpaid yuppies. The guys (and now gals) who, on
their first day of work, put their boss in their sights
and vowed (silently) to have his job in a year (and
their boss's boss's job the year after that). They
planned on getting rich, they planned on attaining

Old Lion wealth, but they were going to be younger when they did it. And there wasn't going to be a little old society lady in black on their arm, either. They had no plan to buy a Corvette. They were headed straight for the Ferrari dealer.

Jillian looked around at the crowd and saw that it was mostly made up of the young wannabes. They were the guys who didn't think the hors d'oevres were too pretty to eat—they wolfed them down—not caring that they were spilling cocktail sauce on their thirty-five-hundred-dollar suits. When someone spotted that the bartenders were pouring eighteen-year-old scotch that retailed for a hundred and twenty-five a bottle, consumption increased dramatically . . .

Spencer held a glass of it himself as he talked to three yuppie sharks who were hanging on his every word. They may have been predators who would eat you alive in the arbitrage market, but they were still little boys at heart and they were getting to talk to, to hang out with, a genuine, honest-to-God spaceman.

"You're sitting on top of what amounts to a fifteen-story building packed with high explosives . . ."

"Cool," said one of the sharks, slugging back about twenty-five dollars' worth of single malt.

"Then what?" asked another of them.

Spencer laughed. "Well, that was the part that none of us ever could figure out . . . After they strap you in, anyone with any sense backs off the gantry by about three miles."

"Then what?" the third one asked. "What happens then? What does it feel like?"

"You feel your first kick after the main engines spark," said Spencer. "But then the solid rocker boosters come on and that's when you know you are about to go someplace very fast."

"Zoom, zoom, zoom, huh?" said one of the wannabes, crunching an ice cube between his very white teeth.

Spencer nodded and smiled slightly. "That's about it . . . zoom, zoom, zoom."

"Man," said one of them, "I'd give up my 401k to go for a ride in a spaceship."

"But you are," Spencer replied simply. "You're riding in one right now."

"I am what, right now?" they guy asked, looking puzzled by Spencer's enigmatic observation.

"You're on a spaceship," Spencer replied. "We all are. That's what the earth is. A spaceship."

"I mean a real spaceship," the guy said. "None of that Whole Earth Catalogue stuff. I want to ride in the shuttle. I want to feel those rockets kick in. Zoom out to outer space."

Spencer shrugged. "Shuttle? Earth? What's the difference? The Earth is a real spaceship. And believe me—we are in outer space right now."

One of the yuppies looked around at the rich crowd, the vaulted ceilings of Fifty-five Wall Street and laughed. "You know, it's not quite what I expected. Though I think I've spotted a couple of alien life forms here."

Spencer smiled thinly. "Space is never what you expect it to be. Never."

One of the first wives who had not yet been dumped by her newly rich husband—and who looked like she expected the news at any minute—had button-holed Jillian. She was a rather dried-up woman with a plummy accent and in an attempt to compete with a host of younger women she had dieted and ex-ercised herself down to mere skin and bone. Jillian remembered something that she had once heard an old black Floridian woman say about someone else: "She's as thin as six o'clock." That sort of summed up this woman.

Jillian was wondering why she was even on this woman's radar. What she did not know was that it was social death to stand alone at one of these func-tions. Jillian was just a port on her way to some place more socially acceptable.

"I used to be into AIDS," the woman was say-ing, "but it got so crowded with the wrong sort."

"Really?" Jillian said, wondering just what the hell this old socialite was talking about.

"Really," she said emphatically. "It just became too, too trendy, you know."

"I see," Jillian replied.

The woman made no secret of the fact that she was scanning the crowd over Jillian's shoulder, searching among the party-goers for a greater social catch. Her hunt for someone else to talk to was so obvious that it made Jillian nervous. She took sip after sip of her drink and wished that someone would come along and rescue her from this extremely awkward situation.

"So I gave up AIDS," she said, her eyes darting back and forth. "And now I'm into hunger."

Jillian felt that she had to say something. "I teach," she said. The Armacosts' move had, providentially, coincided with a shortage of school teachers in New York. With her credentials from Florida and glowing recommendations from her former superiors, Jillian had been welcomed into the New York City school system. It was the one thing in her life that seemed normal, even if some of her pupils had names like Ahmed, Jesús, and Ang. Kids were kids and Jillian just loved being with them.

This admission elicited a faint flare of interest from Jillian's companion. "You teach? Where abouts? At NYU? Columbia? Or do you commute up to Yale in New Haven?"

Jillian smiled. "No, not quite anything as grand as that. I teach second grade."

The woman smiled, too. "I'm sorry," she said, "I thought you just said you taught second grade."

Jillian nodded. "I did. I teach second grade over at—"

But the socialite was looking over Jillian's shoulder again. She gave a little smile and wave to someone in the middle distance. "Ambrose," she squealed. "You look great, darling." She flashed a smile at Jillian. "Marvelous talking to you, dear," she said quickly. "Will you excuse me for a moment?"

But before Jillian could even open her mouth to give her assent, the woman scooted away.

Jillian was not offended, not in the slightest. She was relieved at being left alone. She located Spencer in the crowd and mouthed the words "help me" at him. He immediately broke from the little knot of feral yuppies and started toward his wife, but before he could reach her he was grabbed by a very distinguished-looking man who was carrying a cigar so thick it looked like section of bicycle inner tube. As the man led him away, all Spencer could do was shoot his wife a look that plainly said "What can I do?"

Jillian scanned the crowd and for one terrifying moment she locked eyes with her former companion and it looked as if she was going to have to go over and be introduced to the man known as Ambrose who did not look all that great, Jillian thought. But she dodged that bullet when a woman closer in age to her sidled up to her, drink in hand. She was smiling, plainly reading the social fear on Jillian's face.

"Don't worry about her," said the younger woman. "The total lack of body fat has rendered her something rather less than human. I would doubt if she's had her period for over three years. Which, I guess, is a blessing for the gene pool. Wouldn't you say?"

Jillian smiled and tried to think of something clever to say in reply. Nothing came.

"I'm Shelley McLaren," the young woman said.

"I'm Jillian Armacost."

"I know," she said with a little smile. "I saw you when you came in with your husband."

Suddenly Jillian understood. "*McLaren*," she said. "Your husband must be—"

"Jackson McLaren." She tossed her head in the direction of the man with the big cigar who had snagged Spencer. They had been joined by two more rich-looking men. They also had cigars. Spencer did not have a cigar and he did not want one.

Shelley laughed. "They all had cigars . . . but Jackson had the biggest cigar of all," she said, pretending to be wistful, as if recalling some far-off days of yore.

She then stopped a passing waiter and grabbed two flutes filled with champagne. She handed one of the glasses to Jillian and they clinked glasses.

Jillian felt she had to make conversation. "This is an amazing building," she said.

"It will be when it's finished, but don't let it fool you," she said with a wink. "It's made entirely of processed cheese." Shelley McLaren sipped her champagne. "I can't tell you how excited Jackson was to get your husband on his board of directors. Apparently there was a real little bidding war for brave Spencer Armacost. Jackson won of course. Because Jackson always gets what Jackson wants."

She looked away from her husband and surveyed the vast space they were standing in and then looked over at Jillian, indicating the giant room with her chin.

"Seems pretty strange to you, I'll bet," said Shelley McLaren sympathetically.

Jillian nodded. "How ever did you guess?" she said laughing. "Does it show *that* much?"

"Don't worry," Shelley McLaren said warmly. "It happens to everyone. And a room like this . . . it's supposed to make you feel the way you do."

"What way is that?" Jillian asked.

Shelley waved her hand vaguely at the high ceiling and the marble columns. "Oh, you know," she said. "It's all designed to make you feel insignificant. No woman would ever have built a place like this. Why do men always confuse size with power." She sighed, as if contemplating the follies of the male species and then took a drink from her champagne glass. "So tell me, have you made any friends in the city yet? It can be difficult, I know . . ."

Jillian shook her head and smiled ruefully. "No . . . not really. Of course, I've made some friends at work, but I don't know them well. It's only been a couple of weeks . . . But there's Spencer, of course. I guess we're best friends."

Shelley's eyebrows shot up toward the vaulted ceiling—this rich, sophisticated woman looked genuinely surprised by Jillian's startling admission.

"Spencer is your husband *and* your friend," Shelley exclaimed. "If I were you, I wouldn't let the other wives get wind of that little fact. If they do, they'll be sure to haul you up on charges. Friendship and marriage aren't supposed to mix in this class stratum. But I guess you can be forgiven for not knowing that yet. But believe me, in time, you'll learn all the rules about that sort of thing."

For the first time since she had arrived in New York City, Jillian threw back her head and laughed. She laughed loud and clear and without a whit of self-consciousness. It felt good to her. And it sounded good, too. People in that vast room looked at her as she laughed, and envied her. Very few people had the privilege of laughing like that. Not in polite society anyway.

Even a slightly jaded sophisticate like Shelley McLaren was taken in by Jillian's honest laughter. "Now that," she said, "I like."

"Like what?" Jillian asked, genuinely mystified. "What do you mean?"

"Your laugh." Shelley said.

"My laugh?" Jillian looked at Shelley McLaren as if she had lost her mind. "What does my laugh have to do with anything?"

"It's an honest laugh," Shelley explained. "And let me tell you, it's been a while since I heard one like that. You weren't laughing because you thought you were supposed to—you were laughing because you heard something you found funny."

"Isn't that why people laugh?" Jillian was frankly surprised by Shelley McLaren's reaction.

"Not in this town, Shelley replied. She drained her champagne glass. "You'd be surprised at the number of phonies you are going to run into in New York, Jillian. Sometimes it can be quite scary. No one means anything they say. The check is never in the mail. The best way to follow up a lie is with another lie."

Jillian frowned. "That's sort of cynical, isn't it. Do people really live that way?"

"It's a cynical town, sweetheart," said Shelley McLaren, sounding like a hard-bitten chick from an old movie. "But you'll get used to it in time. Believe me. I did."

"I don't want to get used to it," Jillian replied. Her voice was as honest as her laugh. "I don't want to be so cynical about everything. Or anything, really."

"Think of it as armor," Shelley McLaren advised. "Kevlar body armor. My husband manufactures it, you know. He's got a factory in North Carolina. Makes a fortune on it. And he sells it to the good guys and the bad guys. How do you rate that for cynical?"

Before Jillian could say anything in reply a waiter scurried up next to Shelley and whispered something in her ear. She nodded a number of times and her countenance darkened. "Okay," she said to the waiter. "You tell Andre I'll be there in a minute, okay?"

The waiter bowed from the waist. "Very good, madame. I'll tell him now."

"You do that," Shelley McLaren snapped. Then she turned to Jillian, smiling as if nothing had upset her. "I have to go," she said. "It seems that there has been some minor disaster in the kitchen. Something concerning burning rum balls and no one on earth, it seems, can take care of it but me and me alone."

Jillian looked surprised. "This is your party? I

though that the bank was throwing it.''

"Absolutely correct, madame," said Shelley laughing. "But Jackson is a majority shareholder in the bank. Hence they want to invest in his company . . . and the party is up to me."

"Oh," said Jillian, feeling like a naive fool. She should have known that. Spencer should have told her about their host and the multi-layered complexities of the evening. "Of course. If you're needed in the kitchen you should go." She paused for a moment or two, then asked, "I could help out, if you need me."

Shelley McLaren waved her off. "Don't be ridiculous. I shouldn't be bothered with it so why should you be? Have another glass of Kristal and forget about the rum balls. That champagne is costing my husband a hundred dollars a bottle. Drink as much as you can—I will, I'm trying to bankrupt him from inside. You know, like an undercover agent or something."

Jillian laughed again. "No you're not. I can tell. You love your husband."

This time Shelley laughed. "I am going to call you and we are going to go out and listen to that wonderful laugh of yours. Yes? Am I right, Jillian?"

"Okay," she replied. She felt as if she had really made a friend, her first one in New York City.

"Good," said Shelley. "I'll hold you to that. Now . . . if you'll excuse me . . ." It was exactly the same thing that the dried-up socialite had said when she had wanted to dump Jillian. When she heard the words her face fell. Maybe she had been wrong about Shelley McLaren. Maybe New York was only interested in her husband.

But it turned out that she was wrong. Shelley walked a few feet, then turned on her high heel and walked back to Jillian Armacost. She looked at her for a moment, then spoke, and Jillian could tell she was speaking from the heart.

"Jillian—can I call you Jillian?"

"Of course," Jillian replied.

"I don't want you to worry . . ."

"Worry? Worry about what?"

Shelley waved her arms, as if gathering the entire vast room up and clutching it to her slim body. "About all of this. Don't worry about it. Don't worry if you never get used to this whole New York society thing. I never did."

Jillian was completely calm. "I'm not worried about it. I'm here because my husband needed to be here."

And Shelley McLaren smiled. "Just remember, AIDS is overcrowded with the wrong people."

Jillian looked right back at her, her gaze not wavering, not even a centimeter. "But hunger is hot."

Shelley laughed and touched her cheek lightly. "You're learning so fast. You are going to be just fine . . ."

Then she walked away, leaving Jillian alone in that strange and alien crowd.

Jillian took her slim flute of champagne into a corner of the vast room and sat down on a black velvet sofa. She took a sip of her drink and thought about how much her life had changed in the space of a few months. It had all been put into motion by that terrible accident that had befallen Spencer a few months before. If it had not been for those few terrifying minutes in space Alex Streck would still be alive, Natalie Streck would not have gone through with her bizarre suicide. She and Spencer would still be in Florida, he would be preparing for the next *Victory* mission, she would still be with her old second grade class . . . Calvin and Sarah under her charge . . . instead of being a neophyte socialite in the big, impersonal social capital of the world, New York City.

It was enough to make her mind whirl. So much had happened so quickly. She was almost scared to think about what would happen to her next.

As she sat on the little velvet sofa, musing on her immediate past and the chances for her immediate future, Spencer walked up to her. He held a flute of champagne in each hand and he swayed slightly on his feet as he looked down at her. It was apparent he had been drinking, but he did not appear to be drunk.

"Is this seat taken?" he asked, looking down at the small patch of black velvet next to her.

"Well," said Jillian, "I guess not . . . I was saving it for my husband, but I don't think he's going to show."

Spencer looked at his wife from head to toe, his eyes traveling the length of her slim body. "Your husband, huh? I'd say he's one very lucky man."

He sat down heavily and handed one of the glasses of champagne to her. "Some men don't understand just how good they have things. They don't understand just how wonderful their wives are. Your husband . . . I'm guessing he's some kind of pig."

Jillian smiled but shook her head. "No, not a pig exactly . . . but recently he's been a bit negligent."

"My apologies," said Spencer. He sounded sincere, as if he really had not realized that he had been neglecting his wife. His brief time in their new adopted city had been even more hectic and disorienting than hers. Now it struck him that he might have been just a tiny bit selfish. "Drink your champagne and feel better," he said.

Jillian put the glass down on the little table next to the couch. "I'm afraid I've hit my limit, Spencer," she said.

"Oh come on," he replied. "Have one more glass. With me. It'll do you some good."

Jillian looked around the room, watching the rich people drink expensive spirits. "You know," she said, "I thought your flyboy buddies back at the base could drink. But it looks like these people have got a real love for the joy juice."

Spencer did not answer. He was looking deep into his wife's eyes, so deeply in fact and with such intensity, Jillian felt slightly uncomfortable and blushed noticeably. He raised his glass and tapped it lightly against Jillian's in a quiet toast.

"To us, Jillian," he said softly.

"To us," Jillian replied, her voice barely rising above the level of a whisper.

They both drank. Spencer took a mouthful, but Jillian merely sipped, barely wetting her lips with the golden champagne. She lowered her glass and touched her brow, suddenly feeling the tiniest bit woozy. She was not much of a drinker, but nervousness in these social situations had made her take more than she was used to.

"Oh . . ." she said. "That's the one that does it. Just one glass too many."

Spencer was still staring at her, but his look had altered slightly, now he was looking at her as if he was searching for something in his wife's face.

"What?" Jillian asked feeling self conscious under the intensity of his gaze. "What is it?"

He did not answer with words. Instead he leaned in and kissed her forehead softly, brushing his lips across her skin. It was the sort of gesture a parent might make if taking a child's temperature. Jillian did not notice the oddness of the gesture.

"Mmmm," she said, closing her eyes. "That's nice."

"Yes it is," Spencer replied. Still looking into her eyes, Spencer let his fingertips brush across the skin of her neck, touching her lightly, as if taking her pulse. Jillian swallowed and closed her eyes for a moment, her head whirling.

Spencer leaned down and whispered in her ear. "Maybe we should get you some air."

There was a dark corner of the vast room, a niche some distance from the bulk of the crowd. The noise of the party echoed in the space like a far-off fair and no words could be clearly heard there. There was an occasional burst of laughter, nothing more. It felt very strange to be alone and yet so close to such a large throng of people.

Jillian and Spencer faced each other, very close together. Spencer put his hard, powerful hands up, resting them lightly on the soft bare skin on her shoulders.

"Feel better?" he asked.

Jillian took a deep breath. The air seemed cooler in this dark corner of the room and it cleared her head a little. "Yes," she said, nodding. "A little better . . ."

Spencer held her gaze with his eyes, then allowed his hands to slide down her arms until his fingertips were touching her slim wrists. She did not notice that his index fingers touched her pulse for a moment or two before entwining his fingers with hers.

"Spencer . . ." Jillian whispered.

Her husband silenced her by putting his lips to hers and kissing her lightly. Then he moved his mouth close to his ear and whispered softly to her.

"There's something I need to tell you, Jill," he said quietly. "I have to tell you something about what happened back then. Something about those two minutes . . ."

Jillian was surprised and her eyes widened. "But . . . you never talk about it."

"I want to now," he replied. He smiled softly. "I guess I've had enough champagne to loosen my tongue."

He unclasped his hands and held her palms in his. Their bodies were very close, but they were not touching. Jillian wondered what he would say next.

Spencer's voice never raised above the level of a whisper. "After the explosions, our suits began to shut down. The lights went off. The radio went out. It was black. Silent." He sighed heavily and seemed to shiver. "All there was . . . was the cold, Jill. A cold like you have never experienced. No one has, no one had before as far as I know and has lived to tell about it. Alex and me are the only two."

His hands moved from her palms to her hips, as if looking for warmth.

"But I know what that cold was, Jill," he whispered. "It was death. Death had taken hold of me."

Suddenly Jill had tears in her eyes. The thought of her husband actually dying was too horrible for her to contemplate. Dying out there, as Natalie Streck had said, *alone* . . .

"And then," Spencer said, "it must have been after the first minute or so, the cold began to fade and I began to feel . . . warmth." His hands slid down the hem of her dress, his fingers stroking the inside of her thighs. She put out her hands to stop him, grabbing him by the wrists and looking around worriedly as if someone might see them. But they were in the shadows and far from the crowd.

"I knew what that warmth was, Jillian," Spencer whispered. "It was the warmth of you." He slid one hand higher, working his way up her thigh. This time she let him do it. His other hand held hers, tight and intense, as if trying to telegraph something to her through their interlaced fingers.

"I felt the warmth of your body. I felt the warmth of your hands, Jillian . . ." His hand inched higher. "I felt the warmth of the inside of your mouth." He leaned forward and kissed her. But it was not a paternal kiss on the forehead; this time he opened his mouth and thrust his tongue up against hers.

He moved his hand further up her leg, his fingers brushed the edge of her panties.

"I felt the warmth inside of you," he said. He pushed aside the silky material and slipped his fingers into her, feeling the slick warmth between her legs. Jillian gasped and her mouth opened, her head tilted back, leaning against the cool marble.

"Oh, Spencer," she said breathlessly.

Beneath her dress, Spencer's hand moved slowly, working in and out of her. "Your warmth, Jill, I felt it all around me." They kissed again and she found herself giving in to the hot sensations that were washing through her. She let herself go in the moment and her legs opened and she pushed back against his hand. In rhythm with the thrusts of his fingers her hips swayed and rolled and she could feel the passion growing from somewhere deep inside her . . .

"Oh, Jillian," Spencer whispered.

9

It was as if Spencer's finally breaking down and talking about his brush with death had worked on him like an aphrodisiac. Their lovemaking that night in their big new bed started intensely and then gained in fervor.

Spencer lay between his wife's legs, thrusting into her with a wild passion, grinding, penetrating her, his buttocks working hard like a machine, pumping into her without thought or tenderness. Jillian's eyes were hazy and filmy as if she had been drugged. Her lips were dry, her mouth parched. She tried to raise her head but it fell back on the pillow, as if her neck was not strong enough to support it. As she slumped backward, Spencer's thrusts increased, redoubling his efforts, as if the sex had taken over his brain and he was working on pure animal instinct, as if taking her as deeply as possible was the only thing on his mind, something he was *driven* to do.

Through her foggy brain, Jillian suddenly realized that this was the first time they had made love since the incident in space. And it was not the way they had done it before. Spencer had always been a tender, considerate lover and she had worshipped him for it.

"Spencer," she said weakly, trying to slow him down. "Spencer, what . . ."

But Spencer bore down harder on her and put his lips to her ear. "Jillian," he whispered even as he thrust into her even harder, "Jillian . . . Jillian . . ."

Jillian tried to speak through haze, but her throat was dry and the words were hard to form on her lips. "Spencer," she managed to gasp, "I can't . . ."

Spencer was whispering her name over and over but as he spoke the words in her ear became garbled and then changed to a meaningless gibberish. Jillian raised her arm—it felt like it was attached to lead weights—and put her hand to the side of his face. "Spencer," she said, her voice even weaker now, "Please . . ."

Without halting his powerful thrusts into her, Spencer covered her eyes with his hand. Somehow Jillian felt that the blackness was impenetrable, the darkness shooting through her and overwhelming all of her senses.

In the darkness the sounds of their lovemaking seemed to fade away, but the sound of Spencer's garbled, unintelligible chatter continued to susurrating in her ear.

"Spencer?" Jillian moaned.

And now, Spencer's garbled speech changed. It

sounded like the screaming, chattering of a hoard of insects, very far off but certainly audible. The instant she heard it, Jillian felt a bolt of fear shoot through her like a hot bullet.

"Spencer?" she said, her voice full of dread. The distorted insect-like screaming seemed to be getting closer. Spencer did not answer, but kept his hand over her eyes and thrust into her with even greater vigor, pounding away at her without cease.

The horrible shrieking seemed to fill her head and she tried to shake her head to throw the sound out of her mind. "Please, Spencer?" she said. "Please . . ."

The noise continued but suddenly Spencer had stopped. She felt him shoot into her, a hot streaming orgasm that seemed to fill something in the center of her being.

Jillian found her voice and she screamed. "*Spencer . . . !*"

Jillian awoke—or, at least she thought she was awake. She was in the bed, naked, alone. But gradually she came to realize that the bed was not in the bedroom. All around her, above her, to the side of her, behind her were stars, millions and millions of stars, as if she were trapped inside a dark dome of stars.

Her eyes were open and she tried to raise her head, but she could not. And then, coming from far away, came that sound. The screaming, chattering shriek, but coming closer and closer . . .

*   *   *

Jillian awoke. She was in the bed, naked and alone. She was sprawled on top of the sheets. Startled by her own nakedness she grabbed at the blankets and pulled them around her as if for protection. Slowly she explored her body. There were bruises on her ribs and shoulders where Spencer had held her tight. She put her hand between her legs and winced in pain when she felt her genitals. They were hot and the pain was raw, as if she had been whipped there.

She sat up on her elbows and looked around the shadowy room. Spencer was not there. The apartment was quiet and seemed to be as still as the night. But she listened in the darkness, intently, her ears picking up a faint sound. It was a very small sound and it was emanating from one of the rooms of the house. The sound was small, soft but very clear. Jillian trembled when she heard it—it was no ordinary sound, it was *the* sound. That horrible shriek like a cloud of insects.

Jillian swallowed and gathered up all her courage. Pulling the covers around her, Jillian climbed out of the bed and left the bedroom, walking down the long hall toward the sound. It was still soft, but plainly present. She crossed the dining room, approaching the double doors that led into the living room. The sound was a little louder now. Jillian could feel her heart pounding in her chest. Her breathing seemed very loud, as if it could be heard yards away.

She stood in the door of the living room and saw Spencer on the far side of the room. He was sitting in a chair by the tall windows. On the end table next to him was a small AM/FM radio and Spencer was leaning toward it, as if anxious to catch every sound, every note coming from the tiny speaker.

Somehow he sensed her standing there and quickly, but not frantically, he turned off the radio. That soft, distant insect sound stopped abruptly. He turned and looked at his wife. She was leaning against the door frame, the covers clutched at her throat. She stared at her husband, as if trying to focus on him.

"Spencer," she said, her voice groggy and fatigued. "What are you doing?"

He stood up and walked toward her. "I couldn't sleep," he said calmly. "So I came out here. I was just listening to some music on the radio."

He slipped his arms around her and held her close, feeling her body through the blankets.

"Jill, I . . . I might have had too much to drink tonight and . . ." He swept a hand through his hair. ". . . Well, it had been so long since we made love. If I got out of hand there, I'm sorry. It won't happen again. I promise."

He kissed her softly. "Forgive me?"

Jillian nodded. "Oh . . . I feel so awful," she said. "I think I had too much to drink tonight, too."

Spencer put his arm around her shoulder and started to lead her back toward the bedroom. "Come on," he said gently. "let's get you a couple of aspirin."

As they left the living room, Jillian glanced over her shoulder and looked at the radio. It was sitting silently on the table, bathed in the moonlight coming in through the window.

Spencer carefully remade the bed and then put Jillian in it, like a parent settling a child for the night. Then he went to the bathroom and got his wife two aspirins and a glass of cool water. He handed them to her and stood over her, making sure that she took her medicine. Jillian put the pills on her tongue, then took a couple of gulps of water.

"There you go," Spencer said. "Those will help with the hangover in the morning."

"Thank you," she said, as if thanking a stranger.

He took the glass from her, set it on the bedside table, then climbed into bed with her. He snapped off the bedside light and then cuddled up next to her.

"Good night, Jillian." He kissed her softly, then closed his eyes, dozing off, his arms around her.

There was no sleep for Jillian. She lay in the dark, her eyes wide open, feeling a vague fear.

10

Spencer had left for work by the time Jillian awoke. She was pleased to realize that she had no hangover, no effects from the evening before except for a slight soreness between her legs. That, she knew, would go away.

Bright sunlight flooded into the apartment and it raised Jillian's sprirts just enough to get her out of bed, into the shower, dressed, and ready for work.

As she was about to leave for her job, she noticed the radio, still sitting on the table as it had been the night before. Jillian walked over to it, stopped, and looked at it for a moment, then took a deep breath and reached out and turned it on. From the speaker came some tinny-sounding pop music. Just pop music . . .

"So much for that," she said aloud in the empty apartment. She turned the radio off and left.

The second graders sat at their desks hanging on Jillian's every word. It was the best time of the day—it was story time. Jillian read beautifully, putting real emotion behind the story. And today's story was a favorite, a real crowd pleaser because it called for a considerable amount of audience participation.

". . . Then she began to guess the little man's name," she read, making her voice sound sad and far away. " 'Is it Conrad Pepper Mill?' she said. And the little man said . . ." Jillian glanced expectantly at her students.

"No!" they shouted in unison.

" 'I know, I know!' " Jillian read aloud. " 'Is it Sir William Doorknob?' And the little man said . . ."

"No!" the class yelled again.

" 'I have it,' " Jillian said, clapping her hands. " 'Your name must be Little Ribs of Beef.' And the little man said . . ."

"No!" they all shouted.

" 'It couldn't be Rumpelstilskin could it?' " Jillian said. " 'What did you say?' cried the little man. 'I said, it couldn't be—' "

And the whole class shouted. "Rumpelstilskin!"

"And the little man screamed," Jillian said.

The entire class screamed with glee.

"And he stamped his little foot," Jillian concluded.

Pandemonium erupted in the classroom as two dozen second graders screamed and stamped their feet. Jillian did not do either. She sat on her little chair, the book closed in her lap, her mind far away, thinking of other things.

School was over by two o'clock and Jillian was faced with returning to her empty apartment. In order to delay the inevitable, she lingered in the teachers' lounge, working through the few papers that been placed in her cubbyhole.

As she absentmindedly scanned a school calendar, something changed in her mind. The words vanished and all she could see was a street, a street unknown to her. It looked like New York City, but she couldn't be sure. And she had no idea why the image had sprung, unbidden into her mind.

Jillian had no idea how long she had stood like that, transfixed by this image. She heard someone speaking to her.

"Jillian? Jillian?"

It did not break the spell.

"Jillian? Jillian? Earth to Jillian." Then she slid out of it. Another teacher was peering at her curiously.

Jillian shook her head. "I'm sorry," she said, feeling foolish. "My mind was a million miles away."

"At least," said the other teacher.

The bright sunlight was gone and the dark sky did nothing to make Jillian feel any happier. It was getting later and later and still Spencer had not come home from work. She did not think about eating or anything else. Then, impulsively, she picked up the phone and called her sister Nan, back home in Florida.

Nan caught the nature of Jillian's mood immediately. "Oh God, Jill," she said, "you sound so sad."

Jillian sighed and without thinking about it, reached out with her free hand and touched the radio.

"It's just this city, Nan," she said. "It . . . it just gets inside you. Under your skin."

"Well, don't let it get inside you," said Nan firmly. "That's how you got into trouble after Mom and Dad died. To be honest, you sound now the way you did then."

Jillian did no answer. She realized that she was holding the radio and she stared at it.

"You know, maybe it wasn't such a good idea," Nan continued. "The two of you moving up there to New York City. Maybe it's too much. Culture shock, you know?"

Jillian looked away from the radio. "Spencer needed it," she replied. "And I wanted to do it."

"How is Spencer?" Nan asked archly. "Is he taking good care of you?"

Nan had always been slightly jealous of her sister and her apparently perfect relationship with her apparently perfect astronaut hero husband. She did her best to conceal her jealously, but both sisters knew it was there. By unspoken agreement they never talked about it, though Nan was not above making some sly jokes about it from time to time.

Jillian was silent for a moment. "Well . . . you know, it's not easy for him, either. A new job, so many new people. But you know him, Nan, he never complains."

Nan laughed. "You want me to come up there and kick his ass?" Then she was silent a moment. "Oh, Jilly," she said sorrowfully, "you seem so sad."

"No," Jillian answered quickly, trying to force some the brightness she did not feel into her voice. "No, not at all. I'm okay, Nan. It's just so different up here. It takes some getting to used to. I guess we underestimated how much."

Nan appeared to believe this or decided to pretend that she did. "Have you found made any friends up there? Have you found someone to talk to yet, at least?"

"Oh yeah," said Jillian. "The doorman is a real chatterbox. Can't get him to shut up."

"That's not what I mean," Nan replied, "and you know it. Have you found a doctor to talk to?"

"No . . . Not yet," said Jillian slowly.

Nan sounded deadly serious now. "Promise me, Jill. If things get bad. If they get the way they were before, you have to promise me that you'll find someone to talk to."

Jillian turned as she heard Spencer's keys sliding into the lock in the front door.

Nan was insistent. "Jilly? I want you to promise me that? Okay? Promise?" Because if you don't—"

Jillian cut off her sister. "I have to go. Can I call you tomorrow, Nan? I'll call you tomorrow, okay?"

But Nan would not be put off so easily. She tried desperately to keep her sister on the phone. "No,

Jillian," she said quickly, "don't go, okay? We have to talk."

Jillian looked down at the radio on the table, then toward the front door of the apartment.

"Jillian?" said Nan.

"I really have to go now, Nan," said Jillian.

She heard the front door open and the tap of Spencer's footsteps in the hallway.

"Jillian," he called. "Where are you?"

Jillian put down the phone as Spencer walked into the room. "Spencer," she said. "You're so late . . . I was beginning to get worried about you."

Spencer looked surprised. "Didn't you get my message?" he asked. "I had a dinner meeting tonight."

"I'm sorry," Jillian replied. "I didn't check the answering machine. I didn't think of it."

"My fault," said Spencer. "I still haven't got this corporate thing down yet." He kissed her warmly on the lips. "I'm going to take a quick shower. Will you wait up for me?"

She nodded and he kissed her again. "I won't be a minute," he said, making for the bathroom.

Jillian lay in bed. The light in the bedroom was off, but the door to the bathroom was open. The light was on in there and clouds of steam rolled out from Spencer's shower. Suddenly the water stopped pounding in the shower and Jillian could see her husband toweling off. He was a spectral form in the steam. As she looked into the bathroom, his shadow fell across the bed, across Jillian's body.

From inside the cloud of steam, Spencer called out to her. "You feeling okay?"

Without thinking about it, Jillian placed a protective hand on her belly. "Yes," she said. "I'm fine."

11

Like a high school girl afraid of getting busted for smoking, the next morning, Jillian carefully checked every stall in the girls' bathroom at school. To her great relief all of the stalls were empty and she chose the one farthest from the door, locking it securely. She did what she had to do, then stood up and pulled up and rearranged her clothing. But Jillian did not leave the stall—rather, she stood there for a full five minutes, staring at the small plastic square she held in her hand. Gradually the few drops of urine she had managed to get into the specimen container were searched for something called HCG. If it could not be detected in a woman's urine she was not pregnant and a big black minus sign would appear on the little plastic gizmo. A few minutes after taking the test, the HCG was detected and the mark turned positive.

It was as Jillian had suspected: she was pregnant.

*   *   *

"Do you ever think of what if I had an F-15 in World War II? Or even a B-17 in World War I?" Jackson McClaren asked his dinner guests. "What if you had had a simple handgun in the Middle Ages? Think of the power you would have had. Did you ever think of something as simple as a technology out of time?"

Shelley McLaren replied first. "No, Jackson," she said. "The subject doesn't come up all that often in the circles I move in. We tend to talk about other people."

Jillian and Spencer laughed, but Jackson ignored his wife's snide remark. He always did.

The McClarens were entertaining the Armacosts in the dining room of their Fifth Avenue apartment, an apartment so huge and palatially appointed and furnished that it made Spencer and Jillian's apartment look like a mean and impoverished hovel by comparison.

Jillian could not tell how many servants the McLarens employed—she wasn't sure if she had seen the same one twice—but they moved around the table serving each person, silently and faultlessly. It was almost as if they weren't there at all. It was more that plates arrived and where whisked away by magic. The most astonishing thing to Jillian was how at ease the McLarens were with all this luxury. They took having servants in stride, as if that was the way things were meant to be, one human being serving another.

McLaren was still on his subject, warming to it as he expanded on it. "Think of having an F-15 in

September of 1940. One airplane would win the Battle of Britain. And would do it in a matter of minutes. Think of it.''

"I did once think of what it might have been like if I had been a nun and lived an impoverished life in the service of others," said Shelley McLaren. "The thought lasted about a minute and a half as I recall. Maybe less."

Jackson ignored his wife once again. "What kind of ass could you kick with that type of advanced technology. It would be amazing, truly amazing." The tycoon seemed particularly taken with Jillian and appeared to be talking directly to her.

"Tell me, Jackson," said Shelley, "just how many kinds of ass are there?"

This time Jackson McLaren *did not* ignore his wife. He chose from the cluster of glasses in front of his plate, a rich red claret and took a deep swallow.

"There are many kinds of ass, love," he said, "but on the modern battlefield they are all electronic." He raised his glass to Spencer. "And the fighter this man helped us design can detect, sort, identify, and, believe it or not, nullify anything electronic."

McLaren leaned toward Jillian as if he was going to let her in on a great secret. "Jillian, dove, the modern battlefield is a blizzard, an invisible electronic blizzard. Tanks, missiles, computers, planes— all humming away, their electronic brains adding to the blizzard."

McLaren smiled slyly. "And into this storm flies our fighter. It doesn't drop bombs, it doesn't shoot missiles. It just sends a signal. A signal like the voice of God. A signal like the Devil's trumpet. A signal that over-fucking-whelms every fucking thing. A signal that turns everything *off!*'' He slammed his hand on the table to emphasize his point and there was the tinkling sound of glass and cutlery being rattled on the table cloth.

''By the year 2013,'' McLaren continued, ''all four branches of the military will be flying our fighter. Three hundred units at 350 million dollars a pop. That's 105 billion dollars.'' McLaren got a faraway look in his eyes. ''One hundred and five billion dollars.''

Shelley McLaren giggled and looked over at Jillian. ''It sounds so naughty when he talks about money, doesn't it? The pornography of big numbers, you know.''

Jackson McLaren went back to his usual habit of ignoring his wife's remarks. ''You want to build a plane, ask a pilot. You want to build a plane that's out of this world, ask an astronaut. So that's what we did. And look what we got.''

Spencer smiled modestly.

''Recite the specs for us, Spencer,'' said McLaren. It was almost—but not quite—an order, as if he was asking Spencer to more or less sing for his supper.

''Come on, Spencer,'' McLaren urged with a laugh. ''For me. Just once. It's so beautiful when you say it. It's like poetry or something. Hell, it's better than poetry . . . and it sure as hell pays better. Don't you think, Spencer.''

Spencer nodded. "Two McLaren engines pumping twenty-five thousand pounds of thrust," he recited smoothly and easily. "Ninety feet long. It stands thirty feet off the hardstand. It has a wingspan of seventy-five feet."

"Fully extended," Jackson McLaren put in, as if the two women were actually wondering about it.

Spencer nodded, as if allowing himself to be corrected. "Fully extended. It will have a top speed of eighteen hundred miles per hour. A ceiling of fifty-five thousand feet. A range of three thousand miles. And a crew . . . a crew of two . . ."

Jillian was staring intently at her husband. She was not mesmerized by this litany of facts and figures, but at the way Spencer reeled them off. It was as if she was not quite sure who he was, as if he had become a completely different person . . . a stranger to her.

"Just two?" Jillian asked.

This time Jackson ignored Spencer's wife for a change. "But the best part, the best part is that the computer system that runs the whole shebang is at least fifteen years down the road. It's out there in the future somewhere but . . . we start getting our dollars today." Jackson McLaren smiled broadly. "Don't you just love the way democracy works? God knows I do." He guffawed heartily.

Shelley McLaren feigned innocence. "I've forgotten, Jackson," she said, "who's the enemy now that we need your marvelous new plane to defend us from?"

"The enemy?" McLaren replied without missing a beat. "At this moment? You are, my dear, you are."

"That's very funny," said Shelley deadpan. "You just wait until I pitch my electronic blizzard . . ."

"And we don't say 'plane,' sweet," said McLaren. "We say 'airborne electronic warfare platform.'"

"How poetic." Shelley and Jackson blew each other a kiss, just to show each other they were just kidding.

"Can I ask a question?" said Jillian diffidently. Something had just occurred to her.

"Of course," said McLaren expansively. "Ask us anything you want."

"The sound . . ." said Jillian. "The signal it sends out. What will it sound like?"

"Oh," said Jackson, "humans can't hear it, dove, humans can't hear it at all."

One of the McLaren servants entered and whispered something in Shelley's ear. She stood up and gestured to her husband. "Come, Jackson," he said. "Our darling daughter Augusta has summoned us to her bedside."

Jackson stood up, too. "Ah, the goodnight kiss. After forking over her allowance, the most important moment of the day." He started for the door with his wife. "Behold the glorious joys of parenthood," he said sardonically.

Once they had left the room, Spencer leaned over, moving closer to his wife. He took one of her hands in both of his and stroked it softly and gently.

"You are so far away tonight," he said. "I don't understand what's going on."

"I'm here," said Jillian hesitantly.

Spencer moved his chair a little closer. "Come on, Jilly . . . I know you. There's something . . . tell me. What is it? There's something on your mind."

Jillian shrugged. "I don't understand any of this," she said bleakly. "I don't understand any of these people. I don't understand anything they're saying. It's like they're speaking in some kind of code I can't break."

"Even me?" Spencer asked.

Jillian looked sad as she nodded. "Yes . . . Spencer, I feel," she shrugged as if not sure of what to say next.

"Lost?" He filled in the word for her. "I know. I do, too. But if we're together we're not lost, are we? We have each other, Jill. Always. You know that."

"Why do you have to build that plane?" She could feel a bubble of anger burst inside her. "The way he talks about it, the way you talk about it. It's not—"

"Not what?"

Jillian looked him square in the eye. "It's not you, Spencer. It's not you."

This time it was Spencer who shrugged. "I've told you. It's just business, Jilly."

"You used to say you'd fly forever," she said sadly, as if mourning the Spencer she used to know.

"You used to say they would have to bury you in the sky."

"They almost did," he replied. "I never want to be that far away from you. I never want to be away from you at all." He moved closer to her and looked into her eyes, deep and searching.

"What are you looking for when you do that?" Jillian asked. "It's like you're trying to read something faint and far off."

Spencer whispered, "What are you hiding?"

"How do you know I'm hiding anything?" Jillian shifted uncomfortably.

Spencer leaned forward and kissed her. "How do I know?" he said. "Because I know you."

Slowly, Jillian took his hand and placed it on his belly. She did not have to say anything. Spencer's dark eyes lit up.

"Yes?"

Jillian nodded. "Yes."

Silently a waiter entered the room and began clearing the table. He was as unobtrusive as possible, but the spell between Jillian and Spencer was broken.

The waiter reached for Jillian's plate and then stopped. Nothing on it had been eaten.

"Did you find your dish unsatisfactory, ma'am?" the servant asked diffidently.

"It was fine," Jillian replied. "I just was not terribly hungry, thank you."

Just then Jackson McLaren returned to the room in time to hear the exchange between Jillian and the waiter. His wife was right behind him.

"Are you sure, dove? Howard usually makes quite a cunning langoustino."

"I'm fine, thank you."

The waiter cleared the plate, the uneaten crustaceans staring up at her like big orange bugs.

"Brandy anyone?" Jackson asked. "Oh hell . . . let's all have one, shall we?"

Shelley looked at Spencer and Jillian. They were still sitting close to one another, they were still hand in hand.

"Jackson," Shelley said softly, "remember when we used to sit close like that?"

"No," said Jackson.

12

"This is going to feel a little chilly at first," the doctor said. She squirted a thick snake of clear gooey gel on to Jillian's exposed, swelling belly. The doctor swirled her gloved fingers through the mound of viscous stuff, spreading it in a circular motion in a specific area on her abdomen. The stuff was a little cold and she shivered under it.

Jillian was lying on a gurney in a curtain-enclosed examining room, the doctor, a precise and thoughtful young woman not long out of medical school, standing over her. Like a good and dutiful husband, Spencer had taken time out from his busy day to attend his wife's ultrasound examination— it was the first of several and he felt that he should be there for it. He stood off to one side, feeling a little like an outsider in a particularly feminine ritual.

Standing next to the gurney was a large gray machine topped by a black-and-white video monitor.

The screen was blank but the machine hummed, ready for use.

The doctor picked up the sound wand from its rest and turned it on. "Well," she said, smiling down at Jillian. "Let's have a look in there, shall we?"

She put the wand on Jillian's belly and navigated her way around her body by watching the image on the screen. The gray and black images that the sound waves outlined inside of Jillian's belly did not look like much to either Spencer or Jillian, but to their physician it was as clear as if reading a roadmap.

She stopped the wand over a confused mixture of colors. "There it is. Let's take a measurement."

"There's what?" ask Jillian peering at the monitor. "I can't make out what it is."

The doctor smiled. "It will come clear in a minute." With one hand she kept the wand on Jillian's belly. With her other she punched a few action codes into the keyboard mounted on the front part of the ultrasound machine. A graph appeared on the monitor image of Jillian's insides and the doctor peered at it.

"Well," she said, "based on the size here I would say six weeks, give or take a few days. Everything looks fine. Embryo is a good size ... well positioned." She focused the wand a little and the distinct outline of a head came into view.

"There," said the doctor. "There's something that looks like something. There's plenty of amniotic fluid. And it has everything it is entitled to at this point.'' She pointed to a spot on the monitor. "See this here?" She was indicating a wavering spot on the monitor screen. "See this flickering?"

Spencer leaned in and pointed at the monitor. "This place here?" he asked.

The doctor nodded. "Yes," she said. "You're looking at the heartbeat of your baby."

Jillian looked at that blurred little spot and felt a great surge of emotion, of love. Tears sprung into her eyes. She could not believe that this little thing was living and growing inside of her. She had never experienced anything like it.

Spencer seemed a little put out, though, unwilling to join his wife in her happiness. "That's the heartbeat?" he said. "Is it supposed to be that fast?"

The doctor smiled. "Let me put it this way . . . I'd be worried if it weren't going that fast." She moved the wand around again, bombarding her insides with sound waves from a number of angles. The images would blur and settle as the wand moved and stopped. "I have to say, Jillian, everything looks just fine."

She was just about to shut down the machine when she stopped and peered at the monitor. "Oh," she said. "That's something. That's very interesting."

She kept one hand on the wand and then began to work the keyboard, her fingers flying.

"What is it?" Spencer asked.

Jillian felt her heart clench as she felt a bolt of

fear pierce her. "Is there something wrong?"

"Wait . . . no, nothing wrong. I'm just not sure . . ." She looked closely at the monitor. "Yes. Look here." She jabbed at the screen. "See this? Here? Next to the heartbeat?"

Jillian and Spencer looked at the screen, but could not see what the doctor was getting at.

"Here," she said. "It's a second heartbeat. See? Two heartbeats." She sounded quite excited by the discovery. "Two heartbeats. It's twins, Mrs. Armacost . . ."

"Twins," said Spencer, as if tasting the word.

"Of course," said the doctor with a laugh, "you know this means that I'll have to double my fee." She laughed a little more and then looked down at Jillian.

Jillian wasn't laughing.

Jillian and the doctor retreated to her office and had a little chat, Spencer waiting in the waiting room.

"I couldn't help but notice that you weren't overjoyed when you discovered you were carrying twins," she said. "In fact, you looked quite distressed."

"I . . . can't say that I wasn't. It was such a shock," she said. "I didn't know what to think." Jillian spoke quickly, but she felt that she was coming off sounding like an idiot.

"Mixed feelings during pregnancy are perfectly normal, Jillian," the doctor said soothingly. "And they are particularly normal when you're talking about twins." She grabbed a piece of paper from a pad and wrote something on it in her careful hand-writing. She pushed the paper across the desk toward Jillian.

"This may help," she said.

"What is it?" Jillian asked.

"It's the telephone number of a support group for women who are expecting twins."

Jillian took the paper and looked at it, but the number seemed meaningless. She felt as if she was beyond sitting around with a bunch of women with distended bellies complaining about swollen feet and midnight food cravings.

But she felt the need to confide in someone, even if it was in this doctor whom she had only met a couple of times before today.

"I've felt so odd lately," she said quietly. "Bad dreams, terrible thoughts . . . loneliness."

The doctor leaned back in her chair, a kindly smile on her face. "Your body is undergoing a tremendous change," she said. "It has been for nearly six weeks now. Massive amounts of hormones have flooded into your bloodstream."

"And that could cause this kind of . . . distress? The strange feelings I've been having?"

The doctor nodded. "It could cause nightmares, depression, anxiety, food aversions, giddiness, even disturbances in your hearing. You understand what's going on with you, don't you? It's quite dramatic, you know."

Jillian sounded a little uncertain. "Well, I know that my body is undergoing changes . . ."

The doctor laughed again. "Undergoing

changes? Basically, Jillian, you are mutating completely. But don't worry about it, women have been doing it for millions of years, your body will know what to do . . . even if you think that you don't.''

Jillian shifted slightly in her chair, wondering if she should go on, telling her doctor everything. It took her only a second or two to realize that she had to say more.

"There's something I didn't tell you, something that should be on my chart. I know I should have, I know you should have known but I just couldn't.''

The doctor's laughter was gone and she looked very serious now. "What should I have known?''

Even after years had passed it was still not easy for Jillian to talk about this subject. "A few years ago,'' she said hesitantly, "after my mother and my father died, I had a . . . I had a bad time of it. The whole thing was just awful.''

"How bad?'' the doctor asked. "How awful?''

"It was really strange. I would see people I knew . . . friends of mine, my sister, people I worked with . . . I couldn't help myself. When I saw them I would see them—'' She stopped, not sure she could bring herself to say anymore.

But the woman facing her across the desk seemed to be able to read her mind. "You imagined they were dead?'' She opened Jillian's file and clicked her ballpoint pen.

It was hard for Jillian to admit, but she nodded yes. "That's exactly what happened.''

"Did you seek treatment?'' She took notes as she

asked the questions and that unnerved Jillian slightly.

Jillian nodded again.

"Were you hospitalized?" More notes.

Jillian nodded once again and then looked down at the floor, as if ashamed of her troubled past.

The doctor nodded toward the waiting room, indicating Spencer who was pacing back and forth in an imitation of the classic expectant father mode.

"Does your husband know?" the doctor asked. "Or was it before you met him?"

Jillian smiled. "Oh no, Spencer was in my life then. He knew all about it. But he was the one who got me through it." She was silent a moment. "My husband saved me," she said solemnly. "Spencer saved my life."

"And you're afraid your pregnancy is going to bring all that back? Is that it?"

Jillian nodded again. "I'm terrified of that happening," she said. "It can't happen again. I wouldn't be able to stand it. I don't think Spencer could get me through it again. Not even Spencer could do it and he can do just about anything."

The doctor sighed, stood up, and walked around her desk and put her hand on Jillian's shoulder. "Go to the support group, Jillian," she said. "Spend time with Spencer. Make sure you go through this together. Now that you know these feelings you've been having are caused by the life growing inside of you, by your body adapting to carrying that life . . . cherish it." She hugged Jillian.

"And if you need to, call me, Jillian, any time of the day or night, okay?"

Jillian nodded. "Okay," she said with a nod.

"And if I don't hear from you, I'll see you in a month for your next checkup. Eat well, rest, exercise, and . . ." She cocked her chin at Spencer. "Let him spoil you. Get it while you can—they're lambs on the first one. They want to spoil you rotten now. Wait until it's just an old-hat third pregnancy."

"I'll bear that in mind," said Jillian, feeling a little better.

The doctor said to exercise so Jillian was determined to exercise. Too much rich food and alcohol consumed since arriving in New York City had made her feel fat and out of shape. She was determined to be as healthy as possible for her twins.

It is a little-known fact that many of New York's older buildings—doorman-attended buildings built before the Second World War were deemed the most desirable in a hot real estate market—were equipped with swimming pools. Up and down Park Avenue and Fifth Avenue were apartment houses that were the last word in luxury when they were put up in the twenties, and that meant that they had to have mosaic-encrusted gyms and pools in their basements. Few were in use now—the basement pool and fitness rooms were dank and dark compared to the modern health club.

It happened, however, that the swimming pool in the basement of Spencer and Jillian's building was still there and well maintained, even though it was little used by the tenants. Many newly pregnant women are self-conscious about their bodies and Jillian was no exception. She decided to use the private pool conveniently located in the basement of her own home.

There was no one down there that morning and she was happy about that. There was an observation deck overlooking the pool and that was deserted, too. She stood on the edge of the pool for a moment, took a breath, and then dove into the water. It was just cool enough to be exhilarating, tinged with enough warmth to make the water comfortable. Jillian didn't overdo it, but she swam easily, arm over arm, cutting through the water, swimming the first couple of laps with ease. As she swam she felt good, better than she had in some days—she was calm in the water, listening to her own easy breathing and the regular splash of her feet.

Then Jillian touched the far edge of the pool. She pulled her head out of the water and saw that the pool, the concrete, and the mosaics, the observation deck—everything that had been there a few minutes before—had vanished. She wasn't in the pool anymore but alone and naked lying on her bed.

It was just as before. The bed was hers, but the room was not there and she was surrounded by a spangling of stars and the blackness of space. It was the dome of stars that she had experienced that terrible night those weeks ago.

Her eyes were open and she tried to raise her head, but she could not. It was as if she was paralyzed and drugged . . . Then she heard it. That horrible sound. The insects. The screaming . . .

It seemed to take every ounce of strength she could muster, but she did manage to turn her head. She saw Spencer standing by the side of the bed. He smiled down at her. She wanted to speak to him but could not. Her lips were dry, her throat closed tight.

Slowly and with some grace, Spencer sat down on the edge of the bed, reaching out to stroke her hair gently.

That was when Jillian awoke with a start. There was no more space, no more stars, just the familiarity of her bedroom. She turned in the bed and looked at Spencer. He was awake and looking back at her, a look of concern on his face.

"Spencer," she said, her heart still pounding, her breath shallow. "I don't know what's going on . . . I dreamed I was swimming in the basement pool and then—"

Spencer rolled over and held her close. "Just a nightmare. Shh, shh, shh . . ." he whispered. "You were very upset and were talking in your sleep."

"What was I saying?" Jillian asked.

Spencer shrugged. "I couldn't tell. You weren't really using words. Just sounds, really."

"I'm scared, Spencer," she said softly. She sounded small and defenseless.

"It would be strange if a first-time mother weren't scared, Jillian," he said reassuringly. He leaned over and kissed her. "Come with me," he said, staring to pull her from the bed.

"Where are we going?"

"*You* are going to take a bath," he announced.

"A bath? Spencer, it's the middle of the night."

"So what," he replied. "It be soothing. It will help calm you down."

So that's what they did. Jillian got into a nice warm bath, luxuriating in the giant tub, the scents and soaps that Spencer had poured into the water soothing, almost intoxicating. He knelt by the side of the tub, fully clothed, a washcloth in his hand, bathing her. It was at once both a fatherly and submissive posture.

"Feeling better?" he asked.

Jillian stretched in the water and touched her belly. "Yes," she said. "It's going to be okay, isn't it?"

Spencer dipped the washcloth in the warm water, wrung it out, and brushed it across her taut shoulders. "Yes," he said. "Everything will be fine."

"And we'll be together?" Jillian asked, like a child begging to be reassured that there were no monsters under her bed after awaking screaming from the web of a nightmare.

"Forever," said Spencer.

She put both hands on her belly. "And they'll both be healthy, right?"

Spencer nodded again. "They'll be healthy. And they'll be beautiful, just like their mother."

Jillian smiled shyly at the compliment. "And what will they be when they grow up?" she asked.

"What will they be?" said Spencer. "Of course it's up to them, but . . . pilots perhaps?"

"Just like their father," she said.

Spencer leaned over and kissed her then looked into her eyes. "You are more beautiful than ever . . . Now lean back so I can get to your hair."

"It's like you're my slave," said Jillian, not quite believing his behavior.

"Yes, mistress," he said. "I am here to serve."

Jillian leaned back in the tub and laughed. "Am I dreaming, Spencer?"

Spencer shrugged. "I thought I was. Maybe we both are. It's possible, I suppose."

Jillian slipped a little down the tub, her ears under the water. She looked up at him as he worked shampoo into her hair, his fingers massaging her scalp. All sound was muffled. The only thing she could hear was the beating of her own heart.

13

The first mother of twins said, "For the first three months I was pregnant—every time my husband touched me, I threw up. True. I'm not making it up."

The other women laughed. Some of them nodded knowingly and looked a little sad.

A second woman chimed in with her tale of woe. "I'm okay during the day—really. Just fine. But at night I have the worst thoughts about them. I lie in bed tormenting myself for half the night. Are they still alive? When did they last move?"

A third: "Yeah . . . I know those sick thoughts. Real sick thoughts. Like I convince myself that *one* of them is dead and the other one is alive. In there . . . you know, with it."

It was not the sort of thing she would have done under normal circumstances, but Jillian steeled herself and went to the support circle for prospective mothers of twins. To her great surprise and delight she enjoyed it immensely and derived a great deal of comfort from hearing the stories of others in the same position as she.

There were about a dozen of them and they met once a week, changing apartments every week. Some were older than Jillian, a number were younger; a couple seemed to be richer, but Jillian's husband's position put her in the upper income bracket. They were all in different stages of pregnancy. But they were bound together by a single common bond—they all had two lives growing inside them.

"My husband," said a fourth woman, "he tries to give me that look. You know that 'I understand, honey' look. *Hah!* I don't care how long he rubs my feet, I know he doesn't understand a thing about what I'm going through."

"He rubs your feet?" exclaimed one of the women. The rest of them laughed.

"I know what you mean," chimed in another woman. "We're supposed to be going through this together, but I've never felt further away from him. There's this thing going on inside my body that he knows nothing about."

"Wait, let me get this straight. He rubs your feet? You actually get your feet rubbed?"

All of them laughed again, including Jillian. Her face was lit up, glowing with health. She felt good and happy and she would never tell these women that her husband often rubbed her feet.

"Anyone have memory loss?" asked someone. "This morning I was looking for my glasses . . ."

Another woman filled in the punch line. "And

they were on your face all the time, right? You think that's bad. Yesterday I got into the bathtub with my socks on.''

Before she knew it, Jillian found that a month had passed and she was back at her doctor's office for her next checkup. The support group and Spencer's kindness had helped her enough. She had not needed to call her doctor for assistance, not once. But she had achieved one breakthrough—she now called her doctor by her first name: Denise.

Jillian lay on an examination table while Denise palpated her belly, her finger probing, feeling for irregularities and abnormalities. She did not find any.

"Let me take some blood," Denise said. "Just to make sure that you've got some nice rich blood for the kiddies." She tied a rubber tube around Jillian's upper arm and put a needle into the vein in the crook of her arm. She filled a vial, marked it, and put it in a tray. "Now that didn't hurt, did it?"

"Hardly felt it," Jillian said.

"Want to hear the heartbeats of those two you have tucked away down there?" Denise asked.

"I would love that, Denise," Jillian said. "Can we do it here? In your office?"

Denise nodded. "Yup, with this thing." She held up a stethoscope that appeared to be attached to a small amplifier. "It's a Doppler stethoscope. It picks the frequency of sound waves and that thing"—she pointed to the speaker—"converts them into sound."

"Fine," said Jillian. "Let's do it."

Denise put the membrane of the doppler stethoscope on Jillian's belly and fiddled with a couple of knobs on the body of the machine. Suddenly the room was ripped by the horrible noise—the insect shrieking—as loud as an anguished scream.

Jillian jumped and paled as the noise screamed from the speaker. Denise jumped too and adjusted a couple of knobs. Abruptly the noise ceased.

"What was that?" asked Jillian, still trembling at hearing the sound of her nightmares.

"Just a wrong setting," said Denise. "That was just feedback or something." She could tell that the noise had spooked her patient. "Hey, don't worry about it, Jillian, that sound did not come from you. Here, listen to your babies."

The speaker reverberated with the sound of two heartbeats, rhythmic and sturdy.

"Do they sound healthy?" Jillian asked anxiously. "I mean, they're okay, aren't they?"

"Perfectly healthy," said Denise firmly. She cocked her head and listened for a moment longer. "I'm going to send you to a colleague of mine for an ultrasound."

Jillian started and her eyes widened in alarm. "Why? You've done ultrasounds on me. Why can't you do one here the way you always have, Denise?"

"Hey," Denise replied. "Calm down . . . Jillian, at twenty weeks I send everyone to him. Everything's fine. You are perfectly normal. It's just that he's got specialized equipment; I don't have it here. With the more sensitive equipment we'll be able to get a good look at their spines, count their fingers and toes . . ." She smiled broadly. "It'll be like their first checkup. You'll even get a picture . . . The first one for the photo album, okay? Relax . . ."

It didn't take long for Jillian to calm herself down from the slight shock of the examination and by the time she got home she had convinced herself that her visit to another ob/gyn specialist was just as routine as Denise said it was.

She got even better news that evening when she answered the phone and found that it was her sister Nan—and she had a big announcement to make.

"I'm coming to New York," she squealed.

"Oh, Nanny!" Jillian yelled. "That is fantastic news. Really great. When?"

"Next Tuesday," Nan replied, "that is, if Tuesday is okay with you. I mean if the whole trip is okay with you. You don't mind putting me up or anything. And if you're sure Spencer won't mind."

"Spencer will love it and so will I."

"Are you sure?"

"Oh God yes." Despite the successes of recent weeks Jillian had not realized how much she craved the sight of a familiar face. A visit from her sister was just what she needed. "Nanny, I can't wait. I wish it was sooner. Just wait until you see how fat I am."

"Oh yeah, right," Nan replied. "I'll bet you're that kind of woman that you can't even tell is pregnant when you look at them from behind . . . By the way, is it true what they say about your boobs getting bigger when you're pregnant?"

Jillian giggled. "You'll have to ask Spencer for his expert opinion. He'll know."

"Ooooo, really," said Nan. She laughed happily. "I have to say you sound a lot better, Jillly. In fact, you sound great."

Jillian nodded. "Yeah," she said. "I do, don't I?"

"Okay, sis, I'll see you on Tuesday," said Nan. "Now you have Spaceman kiss your belly for me, okay? You make sure to tell him to do that." ·

"I love you, Nan."

"Right back at ya, Jilly-o."

Jillian hung up the phone happy. She threw herself down on the living room couch, smiling broadly at the thought of her sister's forthcoming visit . . . then her eyes settled on the radio. She looked at it for a moment, then reached out and touched it. Then she turned it on. This time hot, brassy salsa music poured out of the speaker, music with a pounding bass line and heavy beat.

Jillian smiled. "It's just music," she said. And then, not quite knowing that she was actually doing it, she jumped to her feet and started to improvise a mambo. She put her hands on her bulging belly and held it tight, as if dancing with her two unborns. She danced and dipped and spun until she turned and saw Spencer standing in the doorway.

Jillian yelped and stopped dancing. "Spencer! How long have you been standing there?"

"Long enough to see you do the mambo," Spencer replied. "I learn something new about you every day."

"Would you like to see some more?" she asked, starting to sway to the music again.

"You bet."

Jillian danced over to where he stood, put her arms around him and rubbed up against him like a cat.

"Are you ready to serve me, slave?" It had become a joke between them since that night he bathed her. She pushed him toward the bedroom, a lascivious look on her face.

"As my mistress desires," Spencer intoned.

"Oh, I have desires," she said. She took his right hand and put it on her swollen belly. "Can you handle all three of us?"

"As my mistress desires."

She leaned into his face and kissed him hard, then pulled back. "You love me?" she asked.

"Yes."

"You love this big belly of mine?"

"Yes," said Spencer again.

"That's good," Jillian said emphatically, "because I love the big belly, too."

There were no windows in the high-tech ultrasound imaging room that Jillian and Spencer went to the next day. The only light came from the monitor. A technician moved an ultrasound wand across her belly, bare except for the conducting gel that had been slathered on her skin once again.

The increased power of this machine was obvious, the pictures from inside of Jillian's womb were clear and distinct. It took the technician only seconds to find the fetuses.

"There they are," he said. "Right where they are supposed to be. Nice and cooperative."

Spencer and Jillian looked at the dark, shadowy images from within Jillian's body, and fuzzy though they may have been, the two bodies were obvious and alive. They were floating in the amniotic fluid, peacefully waiting their time to emerge.

Jillian had never been so excited. "Oh God, Spencer, there they are." The fetuses seemed to hear her and they wriggled and kicked slightly as if they recognized her voice. "Oh, I feel them moving . . . Oh look, Spencer. Look."

The technician pressed a button on the machine and an instant black and white picture of the twins emerged from a slot, as if from some kind of photomachine one might find at a carnival.

"How's that for a photo op?" the technician asked with a wide grin. "Not bad, huh?"

Jillian showed the picture to her support group the next day. Of course all the other women *oohed* and *ahhed* over it, but it was mostly for Jillian's benefit rather than from any genuine admiration. Most of them had similar pictures in albums or stuck to their refrigerators at home and they had all realized that an ultrasound picture is beautiful only to the parents-to-be. But there was no harm in playing along. They had all done it for others and had had it done to them.

But as Jillian played the beaming proud mother,

a young woman approached her. She wasn't a member of the group but a nanny who worked for the woman who was hosting the meeting this week.

"Mrs. Armacost?"

Jillian looked up. "Yes?"

"I just got a message from your husband," the girl said. "He said that he wants you to meet him on the main concourse at Grand Central Station."

"Grand Central Station?" said Jillian, puzzled. "When?" Of course the more likely question was why.

"He said right now. As soon as possible."

"Did he say why?" Jillian asked.

The young woman shook her head. "No. That's all he said. For you to meet him there as soon as possible."

Of course the traffic on Park Avenue was terrible and everyone and his brother in New York seemed to be looking for a taxi and Jillian had not been living in the city long enough to have begun to have mastered the labyrinth that was the New York City subway system. So she was flustered and frustrated when she pushed her way through the Vanderbilt Avenue entrance of Grand Central Station, stumbling down the stairs to the wide expanse of the Grand Concourse.

The vast room was thronged with rushing commuters and travelers sitting on their suitcases waiting for their trains to be called. Hundreds of feet above the travertine floor was the ceiling, which was painted a deep blue and speckled with golden stars and the figures of the constellations. But the bustling commuters didn't notice it and neither did Jillian. She was too preoccupied looking for her husband.

Near the circular, ornate information booth set in the middle of the concourse, Jillian stopped and scanned the crowd. Next to her a woman played the cello, her instrument case open and littered with currency—everything from quarters to dollar bills. She was working her way through the beautiful suite #1 in G minor by Johann Sebastian Bach. At another time Jillian would have taken pleasure in the music, but she was too busy scanning the crowd for a glimpse of her husband.

Then, suddenly, she felt him, sensed him standing directly behind her.

"I know you're there," Jillian said. She did not turn around to face him.

Spencer smiled. "Now tell me, how do you know that?"

"I can feel you," she said.

"Because we're connected?" As he spoke he reached around her body and took her hands in his. She pulled his hands to her body, cradling her belly.

"Connected," Jillian said, she looked for the words to explain it. "It's like . . ."

"Like what?"

"Like when even we're apart, we're together. It's silly, I know, but I—"

Spencer whispered in her ear. "No, it's not silly. I feel it too, Jill. Sometimes I think I know what you're thinking. Sometimes when I'm at work I close my eyes and I feel as if I can almost see what you are seeing. Feel what you're feeling."

Spencer looked at the ceiling of the station. Jillian looked up, too, the two of them looking at the figures of the constellations painted on that field of gorgeous cerulean blue.

"Can you see what I'm seeing?" Spencer asked.

Julian nodded. "Yes," she said. "The twins."

"Castor and Pollux," said Spencer.

Up there on the ceiling were beautiful renderings of Castor and Pollux, the twin sons of Zeus known as the Dioscuri. The two young men had been brave warriors and great horsemen. To honor their courage and purity Zeus created the constellation Gemini.

"How do you feel?" Spencer asked his wife.

"Like there's a part of you always inside me," she answered. "It's nice. I always know where are."

"Inside you," Spencer whispered.

"Yes, that's right."

The music the cellist was playing changed. She had finished the Bach suite and swung into something a little faster. A big smile on her face, she started to play "Let's Face the Music and Dance." Jillian turned around and embraced her husband.

"Happy anniversary, Jillian," Spencer said. He kissed her warmly and held he close.

"Anniversary?" She put her hand to her mouth and looked worried for a moment. She had completely forgotten that today was their anniversary. She searched for a look of disappointment or hurt in his face. But it wasn't there. He smiled down at her and she could tell that he was secretly glad that he had remembered and that she had forgotten their great date. It was one of those sexual role reversals he loved to pull. He never played the oafish insensitive husband if he could help it. But both he and Jillian had forgotten his brutish lovemaking that had put those twins in her in the first place. But that was in the past and neither of them wanted to dredge it up again.

So she had forgotten their anniversary? So what? For the first time in a long time life was good . . .

14

Never in her life would Jillian Armacost have guess that there were so many products on the market aimed at children not yet born. She walked the aisles of a big store in the East Thirties that catered exclusively to newborns, toddlers, and children up to the age of twelve.

The selection was truly astonishing. There weren't six or ten different strollers and baby carriages on sale—there were sixty, ranging in price from rock-bottom models to ultraluxurious buggies that seemed to cost as much as a small car.

In addition to cribs and car seats, layettes and bassinets, there was aisle after aisle of toys, acres of brightly colored plastic creations catering to every childish whim and fancy.

Jillian stopped in front of an array of plush animals. There were so many of them she felt like she was facing an audience of bunnies and bears, and fluffy elephants and lions and tigers that looked as if they wouldn't hurt a fly, even if they were hungry.

Jillian smiled and picked up two identical fuzzy teddy bears and looked at them. From now on she was going to have to think in terms of twos, two of everything, no playing favorites . . . she wondered if she would be tempted to dress them alike, as mothers so often did with sets of twins.

She was sure of one thing, though. No matter how identical her children might be physically, she knew—she could sense in only the way a mother could sense—that they would have distinct personalities. They would be individuals.

Then everything changed. There was a flash of light before her eyes and she dropped the twin teddies as that image came back to her. That New York City street that she had seen once before. There was something terrifying and distorted about it and she shook her head to clear it. But the image persisted.

Jillian wanted to cry. Things were going so well, she could not allow herself to slip. By sheer force of will she forced her way back to the ordinariness of the kids' store, pushing that cursed street from her mind.

It vanished, and she blinked as if she had just been brought out of a trance by a stage hypnotist. She was sweating and she was scared and she knew she had to get out of there. But as she turned to leave she saw a man standing at the end of the aisle. He was shabbily dressed and carried a tattered overstuffed briefcase. He stared at her and she stared back. And she realized she knew him. It was Sherman Reese . . . well, not *exactly* Sherman Reese. It was a sort of like looking at a threadbare and bedraggled copy of Sherman Reese.

As he took a step toward her, Jillian took a step away, ready to run and scream if she had to.

"Mrs. Armacost?" Reese said. He took another step toward her. "Mrs. Armacost, do you remember me?"

Jillian stopped and forced herself to be friendly. She was in a public place and this man could not hurt her. She rebuked herself for giving in so easily to a hysterical fear.

"Mr. Reese? Is that you?" she said.

Reese walked up to her. "Yes, that's right," he said, his eyes glittering. "Sherman Reese from NASA . . ." He looked her over quickly. She could feel his eyes on her body and it made her uncomfortable. "Are you . . ." He stared at her widening hips and protuberant abdomen. "You're pregnant, aren't you?"

Julian nodded. "Yes, just a few months. I didn't realize that I showed that much . . ." Sherman Reese had always been faultlessly dressed and perfectly groomed. She remembered that terrible day when he had come to collect her to take her to the center where she would await news of Spencer's fate. Even on an awful and disturbing day like that, he had been cool and comfortable. She remembered thinking that his immaculate look had been something approaching an insult to her.

But all that had changed. His clothes were dirty, his shoes scuffed, his tie stained; his once perfectly manicured finger nails were filthy and bitten down to the quick. He wore a three-day growth of stubble on his face. One did not have to be a genius to realize that something catastrophic had happened to Sherman Reese.

"I need to speak to you," said Reese. "It is terribly important, Mrs. Armacost."

Jillian felt her fear and suspicion returning, rising up in her like mercury in a thermometer. "You should call my husband, Mr. Reese. You can reach him at—"

Reese cut her off. "I need to speak with *you*, Mrs. Armacost." He spoke fast and frantically. He spoke in a low and nervous whisper. "I need to talk to you about those two minutes. The two minutes, Mrs. Armacost. You know which two minutes I mean, don't you?"

"What is it, Mr. Reese?" Jillian spoke almost wearily. Things were going so well, but she could tell that the appearance of this odd man spelled the end of that.

Reese seemed overly eager to talk, as if he had been silent for a long time. "Mrs. Armacost, have you noticed any change in your husband's behavior since that shuttle mission?"

Well of course she had, but she had no intention of telling this man about them. Any changes that had occurred in her husband had been explained to her satisfaction. He had been through a horrible and terrifying ordeal. It had affected him. It would have had an effect on anyone. But the shock and the trauma were wearing off now. They were coming out of it together.

"No," she lied. "I haven't seen any change in Spencer. Why do you ask?"

Sherman Reese took a step closer. "It's odd that you haven't seen any changes in him, because I have been going through these files and I see some striking anomalies and peculiarities." He threw open the bulging briefcase and pulled out a thumb-stained photocopy of an official NASA document.

He pointed at a line on the piece of paper with a grimy finger. "Like right here. You see? This is your husband's signature from just before he went on the last shuttle flight. It was a release that all the crew members were required to sign—it's a secret, you know, that they have to sign a release, but they do. Ever since *Challenger*—"

"Mr. Reese . . ."

Sherman Reese realized that he was losing her. "This was the signature that he signed before he left," he said quickly, "and here is a form he signed on his return. I admit, they are similar but they are not the same . . . they are not the same signature."

Jillian did not bother to examine either the before or after documents or the signatures on them. Instead, she frowned at Sherman Reese, looking at him crossly. "May I ask you a question, Mr. Reese?"

"Of course, Mrs. Armacost."

"Are you in New York on official NASA business?'' she asked sharply. Of course, she knew the answer already . . .

Reese chose to ignore the question. He yanked another paper from his packed briefcase. ''These are the results from the medical tests we ran when he got back,'' he said, thrusting another grimy document under Jillian's nose. ''See . . .''

''*Mr. Reese!*'' Jillian almost shouted, cutting him off before he could say another word.

He did a sort of glottal stop and looked at her.

''I asked you if NASA knows what you are doing? Do they know you are here?''

Reese waved his hand dismissively. ''Oh, they wouldn't listen to me. They didn't want to hear. They terminated my employment the first chance they got.''

That was all Jillian needed to hear. ''I have to go now, Mr. Reese. If you have something to say to my husband . . .'' She turned and started to walk away, but he followed her like a puppy.

''All I did was show them the facts and they terminated my employment,'' he said. ''They referred me to a psychiatrist. I told them the facts, Mrs. Armacost, but they could not comprehend it. In fact, they did not want to comprehend it.''

Jillian still marched toward the door trying not to hear, but Reese still followed her.

''Please,'' she snapped over her shoulder, ''Please leave me alone. Stop following me.''

''I've seen Captain Streck's autopsy report, Mrs. Armacost. He died of a massive stroke. His system overloaded. His body could not take the strain.''

Jillian did her best not to hear. But she could not help but hear the next thing he had to say loud and clear. "I've seen Natalie Streck's autopsy report as well," Reese said.

That was enough. Jillian stopped and turned on him, the anger showing plain in her face. "Natalie killed herself, Mr. Reese. She committed suicide. I was there. I saw it."

Reese smiled blandly. "Yes, yes, that's true. She did kill herself. But . . . according to the report . . . when she took her own life she was just three weeks pregnant. Did you know that, Mrs. Armacost? What does that tell you?"

For a moment, Jillian was silent. "What?" she said. "What did you say?"

"She must have conceived just after her husband got out of the hospital," said Sherman Reese. "She was definitely pregnant, Mrs. Armacost."

She knew that he was telling the truth and the truth hit her like a hard punch to the face. Jillian started to back away from him. "I don't want to hear any more," she said.

"But there is more, Mrs. Armacost," he said. "There is much more. What do you think happened during those two minutes, when they were alone? What happened?"

Reese was right in her face now and he had pulled a pocket tape recorder out of his suit coat. He was talking fast. "Did you know the space suits your husband and Alex Streck wore had built in recorders? They tape everything they say, everything they hear." He waved the little black box in her face. "This is a tape of those two minutes . . . those two minutes when they were out of contact."

Jillian stopped and watched, transfixed, as Sherman Reese held the tape recorder high and pressed play.

She heard Spencer's voice first. "I'm going to rotate the main panel forty-eight degrees. You got me, Alex?"

"Spencer," whispered Jillian.

Alex Streck's voice was clear on the tape. "Good to go. I need the 9c spanner as soon as . . ." There was a pause and then Streck's voice came back on the tape. "Spencer? Did you feel that?"

Spencer's voice was filled with fear. "Alex? Jesus. *Alex?* What the—"

Alex's voice ceased and there was nothing to hear but the hiss of the tape running over the heads. In spite of herself, Jillian grabbed the recorder and shook it, as if trying to force more sound our of it.

"You heard Streck?" Reese asked. "He felt something. Your husband felt it, too. And what ever it was, it scared the shit out of them. What do you suppose would do that?"

Jillian spoke as if she was reciting an answer learned by rote. "It was an accident. There was an explosion. The satellite—"

Reese shook his head vigorously. "No. They train for explosions. They train for accidents. They train for hundreds of hours. When something goes wrong they have a plan. They do not panic. They do not deviate. They stick to the plan. That's what they do." Reese lowered his voice. "Something happened up there that those two men did not train for. What could do that to two highly trained astronauts? Something that would scare them like that . . . ?''

Jillian's eyes were wide and she felt fear pulsing in her veins. She started backing away from him, but he grabbed her by the arm and asked the question she had been avoiding herself. ''Can you swear to me he's still your husband? Can you?''

A security guard wandered into the area, aware that something strange was going on here.

''Ma'am, is that man bothering you?''

''Yes,'' said Jillian. ''Yes, he is.''

Jillian pulled her arm away from Reese and pushed by the guard. When Reese tried to chase after her, the man grabbed him and pushed him back. ''Okay, mister, it's time to leave the lady alone. Understand? No more trouble.'' But Reese ignored him.

Sherman shouted after her. ''Please, Mrs. Armacost. There's more. ''There's something else. I have to show you. You have to see it,'' Reese yelled.

But Jillian was running for the exit. She looked over her shoulder once and saw the guard restraining Reese. But the guard could not stop his voice from reaching her ears.

''You know,'' Reese yelled, ''don't you? You already know that I'm telling you the truth.''

Jillian was going to push through the door when she heard his voice for the last time. ''I'm at the Nesbit Arms, Room 323. Please, Mrs. Armacost. Please get in touch with me.''

*   *   *

Then she was outside and standing in the street waving for a taxi. She was still shaking when she got home, but when she put her hand in her pocket for her wallet, looking for money to pay the taxi, she realized she had taken Sherman Reese's tape recorder with her when she fled from the baby store.

Jillian let herself into the silent apartment and went directly to the most private room in the house, a large walk-in closet that led directly off the bedroom. She sat on the floor of the closet and pressed the play button.

Spencer's voice was clear. "Alex? Jesus. *Alex*? What the—" Jillian snapped off the tape reorder. Very methodically, she stood up and took a scarf from a drawer in the closet and wrapped the plastic tape recorder in the material. Then she went to the kitchen and found the hammer they kept in the utility drawer. Then she returned to the closet, sat down on the floor again, and placed the tape recorder in front of her.

She paused a moment, then brought the hammer down on the little plastic box. She smashed it over and over again. And each time she brought the hammer down she said, "*No, no, no, no . . .*"

15

The upsetting events had caused Jillian to lose track of time so when she answered the front door of her apartment and found her sister Nan standing on the threshold, all she could do was stare at her, her mouth open. The effect would have been almost comic were it not for the fact that Jillian looked terrible. Since her bizarre encounter with Sherman Reese she had lost that look of sunny good health; there were blue-gray rings under her eyes, her hair was lank, and her shoulders sloped as if weighted down by some unseen burden.

Nan stood there dressed in bright clothes, a big smile on her face. "I'm looking for the pregnant lady in 18G," she almost shouted. Her smile vanished, though, the instant she got a good look at her sister's gaunt face.

"Oh my God, Jillian. Jillian, what's wrong?" She dropped her bags and the bouquet of flowers she had been carrying and threw her arms around her sister.

"I'm glad you're here, Nan," Jillian whispered. "I am so very glad you're here.

They made some coffee, then settled on the couch in the living room, Jillian filling her sister in on some of the stranger events of the past months. As she spoke, she kept on glancing at the radio on the coffee table, as if it was something like a third set of ears in the room, listening to what she was saying.

She told Nan about her bizarre encounter with Sherman Reese at the baby store.

Nan nodded. She remembered Sherman Reese. She was incredulous, though, at what he had done. "Reese?" she said. "That suit from NASA, he followed you right into the baby store?"

"He wasn't a suit anymore, Nan," Jillian replied. "He was a mess. Dirty. Unshaven. He said he had been fired by NASA, though he called it something else, a sort of bureaucratic term for getting fired. 'Separated my employment,' or something like that."

"What the hell did he want with you?" Nan asked indignantly. "NASA always figured it owned people. I could always feel it when I was around those guys."

"But he's not NASA anymore," said Jillian.

"They get them for life," Nan replied. "What did he want with you anyway?"

Jillian took a deep breath. "He said . . . he said that Natalie Streck was pregnant when she died."

Nan was unimpressed. "Now just how in the hell would he know something like that?"

"He said he had seen the autopsy. He said that she must have gotten pregnant right after Alex came back. You know, after he and Spencer had their . . . incident."

"I know," Nan said as she folded her arms across her chest. "What else did Reese have to tell you?"

Jillian shrugged and looked away, glancing at the radio as she did so. She could not bring herself to say any more. She could not tell her sister about the tape and Reese's suspicions that Spencer was a changed man, possibly a completely *different* man.

Nan read the fear in her sister's face. "Oh, Jilly," she said, "a little freak like that is the last thing you need to worry about. If I were you I would just have Spencer call some of his—"

Jillian cut her off sharply. "No. No, don't tell Spencer I saw this. I don't want him to know."

"But, Jillian," Nan protested, "you yourself said he looked crazy. He might *try* something crazy."

Jillian just shook her head. "You have to promise me, Nan. Promise you won't tell Spencer."

"You can't keep these things bottled up inside you," said Nan firmly. "Carrying a baby requires a completely stress-free existence. Even I know that."

"And telling Spencer about Reese will up the stress levels around here into the danger zone," Jillian countered. "Don't you see? You're right, that freak is the last thing I need. But if Spencer knows about it it'll become a whole big thing. You know how men are, they have to do the masculine thing and protect hearth and home . . ."

"What's wrong with that?" Nan asked. "I think it's nice and old-fashioned."

"Well, it's pretty stupid if there hasn't been a threat to either hearth or home," said Jillian. She smiled at Nan. "Look, if Reese bothers me again, then I'll tell Spencer about it. Okay? Deal?"

Nan relented and threw her arms around her sister's neck and hugged her. "Sure, Jilly, whatever you want. I have missed you so much, Jillian. Too much."

"And I've missed you, Nan." A sad look came across her face like a light squall. "I wish Mom and Dad were still here. There are so many things I want to ask Mom."

Nan forced herself to sound cheerful. "Well, I'm here. Anything you want, just ask. You want me to go and get you a big dish of pickles and ice cream, Jilly, just say the word."

Jillian smiled softly. She glanced at the radio. "I'm okay, right now, Nan."

"You want anything?" Nan persisted.

"Some music," said Jillian. "Just, um, turn on the radio, okay, Nan? I wouldn't mind hearing some music."

"Music?" said Nan. "That's great. You want me to put in a CD. I got a bunch in my pack. Heavy metal German music? It's really cool. I think it's going to be the next big thing."

Jillian shook her head. "No, please, Nan. Just the radio—that will be fine."

Nan shrugged and turned on the radio, soft music of the easy-listening variety came out of the speaker.

"Is this okay?" Nan asked. It certainly wasn't music suited to her tastes.

Jillian nodded yes and closed her eyes . . .

That night Spencer insisted on taking Jillian and Nan out to dinner at one of the more chic downtown restaurants, a place at which Spencer knew he could get a table merely by having his secretary call up the maitre d' and mentioning Jackson McLaren's name. That got them on the list and assured them a table—but it was almost impossible to get a table at one of these places *on time*. The maitre d' invited them to have a drink and said that they would have their table shortly.

There was quite a press of people at the bar, but Spencer managed to elbow his way through the throng and score a drink order without too much trouble.

He passed out the drinks. "Champagne for you, Nan," he said, passing her a flute of golden liquid. "And apple juice for you, Jillian." He handed over a tall glass with ice.

"Thank you," said Jillian taking her drink from Spencer.

"Apple juice?" said Nan. "That looks suspiciously like a bourbon and water to me."

"It might look like bourbon but it is one hundred

percent natural apple juice," said Spencer. "Well, for your information we are having a uncontaminated pregnancy."

"So what's that in your glass, Spaceman."

Spencer smiled. "It's a glass of very pure champagne," he said. He raised his glass. "Welcome to New York City, Nan."

"Thank you, Spaceman," said Nan.

Jillian said nothing. They all sipped, Spencer watched as Jillian drank her juice.

The head waiter approached diffidently. "Mr. Armacost, your table is ready," he said.

It was a good table, a circular booth in the front of the room, a good place to watch the crowd. It was plain that Nan was thrilled to be in a chic New York restaurant and that Spencer was having a good time, too. Jillian was silent, wrapped up in her own thoughts and worries. She let Spencer and Nan spar and flirt and make fun of the other tragically hip patrons in the restaurant.

"So there's no one here that catches your fancy," said Spencer after they had surveyed the men standing at the bar.

"Nope," said Nan.

"Well, I guess that's okay," Spencer replied. "You have your man down in Florida. What's his name? Steve? Sean? Wasn't it something like that?"

Nan guffawed. "Oh. Stan. You mean Stan. Or, better known as the Grand Marshall of this year's parade of losers. Stan's gone. Long gone." She glanced at her sister. "We can't all be as lucky as Jill here, you know. Lightning doesn't strike twice in one family like that."

"I'm the lucky one," said Spencer, reaching for his wife's hand. As he did so a bead of sweat rolled down her temple. Then he moved his hand to her belly. She glared down at his hand, willing it off her.

"Jillian," Spencer asked. "Are you okay?"

"I'm fine," she said. "Just hot."

Spencer picked up her glass of apple juice. "Here, drink some of your juice."

Jillian pushed it away. "I think I want to go home . . ."

She hardly remembered the cab ride back to the East Side, she vaguely remembered undressing and getting into bed. She slept soundly for a while then something pulled her to wakefulness. It was the sound of laughter—Spencer's and Nan's—coming from the living room. She peered at the glowing red numbers of the digital clock face. It was just after midnight, 12:15 A.M. She slept again for a while, but when she awoke the house was silent. Spencer was not in the bed with her, and there was a narrow line of faint light showing under the bedroom door. Jill got out of bed.

Spencer was sitting in the living room, and it was almost completely dark there, the only light coming from a single dim lamp. Spencer stood up as soon as Jillian walked into the room. She looked groggy and tousled by sleep.

"Feeling better?" he asked. She was wearing one of his old soft cotton shirts as pajamas and he reached out to her to do up the top two buttons.

"It's your shirt . . . you don't wear it anymore . . . not since Florida, anyway."

"And why should I?" He place a dry little kiss on her cheek. "Why should I wear it when it looks so much better on you."

Jillian didn't answer but looked around the shadowy room. "Where's Nan?"

"She went out."

"It's after midnight," said Jillian. "And she doesn't know the first thing about this city."

"She's young, Jilly. She's meeting some friends to go clubbing. That's what you do in New York."

"I didn't know she had any friends in New York," said Jillian. "She never mentioned them to me."

Spencer shrugged. "Well, apparently she has. People younger than us. Remember when we were young?"

"Were we?" Jillian asked, a trifle archly.

"Oh yes," said Spencer. "I remember. We used to be up all night dancing on tabletops . . . I remember everything . . ." He got a sly look on his face. "And if you aren't nice to me I'll be forced to tell the twins what a wild woman their mother used to be. You know, back in the Middle Ages . . ."

Jillian did not laugh. Spencer looked into her eyes and found not a spark of amusement or pleasure or even affection there. He sighed heavily and shook his head.

"You were so close there for a while," he said sadly. "But now you are so far away again."

Jillian did not bend. "You ever think about what happened? About Alex? About what happened to Natalie? Does that ever cross your mind, Spencer?"

He shook his head slowly. "Jillian, please . . . Let's not go through that again. I thought we had managed to put things behind us, as if it was all in the past now."

"When you were out there, those two minutes, Spencer, when you almost died . . ."

Spencer groaned, "Why do you want to go back there, Jillian? We're happy here now. We have each other, we have the twins. Nan is here. Why do you want to back to that. I know it's hard sometimes, but can't you try to be happy?"

He held her close. "Just stay here with me, okay, Jillian? Please stay here with me. That's all I ask."

Jillian's voice was very, very soft. "It feels like a dream," she said. "I'm not sure I'm not still asleep."

"You're awake," said Spencer.

"Then I'll try," said Jillian.

"What?"

"I'll try to be happy," said Jillian.

Spencer nodded and smiled. "Good," he said. "Now let's go to bed, Jillian."

Spencer was gone by the time she woke the next morning. She showered and dressed and prepared to go out when she discovered her sister Nan passed out on the living room couch. She was wrapped in a blanket. She wondered if Spencer had given it to her or if she had wandered drunkenly around the apartment during the night looking for and finally finding a linen closet.

Jillian looked down at her sister for a moment and then changed her mind about going out. She decided to stay in and make some phone calls first . . .

16

The phone was answered on the second ring. "Nesbit Arms . . . What?"

"Room 323, please," said Jillian.

"Wait a minute."

There was a moment of silence, then the sound of the extension ringing.

"Yes?" She recognized Sherman Reese's voice instantly.

"Mr. Reese, this is Jillian Armacost . . ." She paused a moment to gather her thoughts and her courage. "The autopsy on Natalie Streck, what did it say about the baby?"

Reese did not answer.

"Mr. Reese?" said Jillian. "Are you there? Mr. Reese? Please speak to me."

Reese's voice slightly louder than a whisper and he seemed to speak through clenched teeth. "Not on the phone, please, Mrs. Armacost. *Not on the phone . . .*"

But Jillian was insistent. "Please, you have to

tell me. What did the autopsy report say about the baby.''

"Mrs. Armacost . . . It is not safe to—''

Jillian's voice rose and she shouted at him as she interrupted. "Mr. Reese! What did the report say about the baby.''

Reese's voice was very soft and quiet. "Babies, Mrs. Armacost. It was babies.''

"What?''

"Natalie Streck was pregnant with twins, Mrs. Armacost,'' he said. "She was carrying twins.''

Jillian felt as if she had been hit in the stomach and it took her a couple of moments for her to digest what she had just heard. "What's happening to me, Mr. Reese?''

"You are, too, aren't you, Mrs. Armacost? You are pregnant with twins, too, aren't you?''

Instinctively she touched her belly and swallowed hard. "Natalie's babies, Mr. Reese, please . . . what did the autopsy say about them? You have to tell me.''

Reese spoke quickly. "There's something I have to show you, Mrs. Armacost. Something you need to see. Do you understand me, Mrs. Armacost?''

Jillian paused a long time. And when she started talking again she sounded like a second grade teacher, light and airy and full of roses and perfume. But she told a story that was hardly fit for the innocent ears of a class of second graders.

"Do you know the story of the princess whose beloved prince dies in battle?'' she asked.

"Mrs. Armacost, I have something you need to see. Do you understand me?"

Jillian ignored him. "The enemy prince, after overrunning the castle, finds the princess and forces himself upon her. Months later the princess is with child. But whose? It's either the child of her enemy, the man who killed her husband, the man who raped her. In which case, she will kill herself and the child. Or is it the child of her prince, the only thing she has left of her beloved, a part of him still alive in her, kept safe in side her. In which case . . . But how will she know until it is too late? How will she know until the child is born and she can see its eyes?"

The enigmatic message got through to Reese loud and clear. "Meet me right now," he said urgently. "Somewhere public. Leave your apartment. Meet me now."

"Where?"

"The subway . . ."

When Jillian emerged from her bedroom she saw that Nan was awake, sort of. She was sitting at the kitchen counter, still wearing the clothes she had slept in, drinking a cup of coffee and nursing a colossal hangover.

Jillian smiled. "Well, don't you look the picture of health this morning."

"Jilly, don't be cruel," Nan muttered. "They certainly like to party in this town."

"Well yes, that's the reputation . . ." She headed for the door. "I've got some errands to run. Why don't you take it easy this morning and we'll do something later.''

The suggestion was music to Nan's ears. "I'll take it easy this morning and we'll do something later. I love it."

"Bye," said Jillian and left.

It was only half an hour later that Nan realized that she had been outsmarted by her sister. She was sure Jillian was going to meet that weirdo Reese. She wondered what she could do about it. She had to stop it because she was sure it was a bad idea . . .

It was Jillian's first ride on the New York City subway system, a simple ride on the Number Six Lexington Avenue Local from the Upper East Side to the stop at Fifty-first Street. Following instructions Reese had whispered hurriedly to her on the phone, she rode in the front car of the train and got out of the station at the exit farthest downtown, the one that led out on to the corner of Fiftieth Street and Lexington Avenue.

When she got out of the car she walked along the platform to the exit, following the grime-streaked tile tunnel that led to the exit stairs and the street above.

She reached the end of the tunnel, pushed through the turnstile and started climbing the stairs. It was a long set and she had to climb a bit before the street at the top of the stairs came into view. She climbed a few more and saw Sherman Reese standing there at the curb, clutching his tattered briefcase, as if he was just another midtown businessman waiting to cross the street. As Jillian rose toward him, Reese looked down at her and half smiled.

She had ten steps to go when she saw a look of absolute shock cross Reese's features. Up there at street level he had seen something that had startled and stunned him so that for a moment he looked as if he was about to make a run for it. Then he seemed to get control of himself and he looked down to the subway steps and shook his head at her—it was a slight but definite movement of his head. It said: "no."

In spite of herself, Jillian took another step or two up toward daylight and once again she was shaken off by Reese, he even risked a little wave of his hand, as if attempting to push her away. This time Jillian stopped dead, her head just inches below street level. She was looking up at Reese when she saw someone else—Spencer walking along the sidewalk just above her. She gasped and retreated a step, flattening herself against the dirty wall, desperate not to be seen by the man she was supposed to be in love with, the man who loved her.

Spencer did not see her, but he had definitely spotted Sherman Reese. He walked straight up to him and tapped him on the shoulder. "Sherman Reese," said Spencer. "Well, I'll be damned. What are you doing here in New York?"

Reese smiled as best he could. "Commander Armacost. What a surprise . . . Of course, you're living up here now. I had quite forgotten about that."

"Really," said Spencer. "I'm as surprised to see

you. I saw you across the street and I said to myself 'Is that Sherman Reese?' So I trotted on over here and yes, here you are.''

Jillian still hugged the wall. She had not retreated at all, but had not gone up a step, either. She could see and hear her husband and if he should happen to look down the staircase he would see her, too. She could feel her heart pattering in her chest.

But Spencer did not look down. He focused all his attention on Sherman Reese. ''Are you in town on business?'' Spencer asked. ''NASA business?''

''I am not with NASA anymore,'' Reese said stiffly, trying and failing to keep the bitterness out of his voice.

Very casually Reese put his briefcase down, placing it just at the base of the concrete railing that encircled the entrance to the subway station.

Spencer nodded and looked sympathetic. ''I had heard that,'' he said. ''I just thought it was one of those nasty agency rumors that crops up every so often. It's sad to see it's true. Should you need a recommendation, I'm the man to ask.''

''I appreciate that,'' Reese said.

Spencer rested his hand on Reese's shoulder. ''You know, it's funny running into you like this. I was just thinking about you, Mr. Reese. Just yesterday.''

''Really,'' said Reese casually. ''That is something of a coincidence. Can I ask what you were thinking?''

''It was about those tests you wanted to do on me after Alex Streck died. Remember those? Look,

Sherman, do you have some time right now?"

"Actually," said Reese reluctantly. "I was just about to—"

Spencer cut him off. "Come on now, Sherman. You're a man of leisure now. You've got nothing but time . . ."

Jillian stood transfixed, straining to hear every word. Then a train thundered into the station beneath her, obliterating all other sound. She saw Spencer lean over and yell something in Reese's ear. Then Spencer took Reese firmly by the forearm and walked him away from the entrance to the subway station. Jillian's heart leaped when she saw the abduction and she almost cried out when she realized that Reese had left his stuffed briefcase behind, resting against the railing of the subway station entrance. It was obvious that she was supposed to take it.

She took a tentative step up the steps, a hand out to grab the case. But before she could lay her hands on it she heard her husband's voice again.

"Forgot your satchel there, Mr. Reese." Spencer leaned down and grabbed the case and then jogged back to Sherman. He had come within inches of his wife, but had not seen her. She waited a moment, then walked slowly up the stairs and stood on the sidewalk. There was no sign of Spencer or Reese. They had vanished into the swarms of pedestrians thronging the streets of the city.

There was a time when the Nesbit Arms would have been called a flophouse or a fleabag. Now it went by the acronym SRO—single room occupancy hotel. It was a dumping ground for the mentally ill, people living on tiny disability checks, alcoholics, drug addicts, and those just hanging on because they knew that the next stop after places like the Nesbit Arms were the cold, unforgiving streets of the city.

It took some courage for Jillian to walk into the place and to cross the dimly lit lobby and to enter the rickety elevator. She got off on the third floor and walked down the narrow hall. Odd sounds emanated from the rooms that lined the corridor. There was laughter, music, screaming, moaning. The whole dispiriting scene was punctuated by the unpleasant odors of cooking, stale beer, and bug spray.

Jillian stopped in front of Room 323. She touched the door and to her surprise it swung open. Quickly she stepped inside. The room was spotless—or as spotless as a room in an SRO can be. The bed was neatly made, the dresser bare. The closet was completely empty—there was not a scrap of paper or a piece of clothing, nothing that suggested that a human being occupied this unpleasant little space. Nothing, that is, except for a single drop of blood on the cracked gray linoleum floor. The reddish brown spot was about the size of a quarter.

Jillian looked up from the floor and into the cracked mirror above the dresser. Looking back at her was the grizzled, unshaven image of a thin old man. Jillian whirled around to face him.

"So," the old guy asked conversationally, "tell me, you a hooker or a cop?"

She was too startled to answer. He looked down at the floor and saw the bloodstain as well. He walked over to it. "I'm the clerk in this place and I don't like people in my rooms who don't belong here. Now . . . are you a hooker or a cop?"

"I'm neither," Jillian managed to say. "I'm a friend . . . of Mr. Reese."

Jillian looked down at the blood on the floor and the clerk put his foot over it, rubbing it with the toe of his shoe. Then he patted his pockets looking for a cigarette. He found one, lit it and exhaled a cloud of bluish smoke.

"Is this Mr. Reese's room?" Jillian asked. "He told me he was staying here."

"His room," said the clerk. "Not yours."

"You're sure this is his room?"

The clerk took another deep drag on his cigarette and nodded. "This is what I do, ma'am. This is all I do. All day long. I keep track of these rooms. Who checks in, who checks out . . ."

"Did Mr. Reese pay in advance?" Jillian asked.

"Mr. Reese still has two weeks left on his advance, ma'am," he said. "He was here this morning. Maybe he'll be back. Maybe not. You can never tell."

Jillian nodded. It was plain that she wasn't going to get anything out of this guy—chances were good he didn't know anything, anyway. As she turned to leave the dingy little room she noticed that there were three brand-new deadbolt locks on the door.

"You find that Mr. Reese of yours," the clerk said, "you tell him he's welcome back here anytime. He pays in advance and not only that"—he fingered the deadbolt locks—"he does his own improvements to the property."

17

The thing that Jillian planned to do with Nan later that day was give her a healthy dose of hell. Spencer's sudden appearance at the rendezvous point between her and Reese was far too convenient to be mere coincidence. Nan—and only Nan—could have tipped him off to Reese's presence in the city.

"You were the only one who knew, Nan," Jillian raged at her sister. "And I asked you not to tell him."

Nan's head was still throbbing from her big New York night out and she was close to tears. "I didn't do it, Jilly," she said. "I swear it, Jilly. Really . . ."

Jillian was unmoved by this display of emotion. "What were you talking about last night, last night when I was in bed. The two of you were out here. I heard you."

"We were just talking," said Nan defensively. "Just shooting the breeze. Nothing more than that."

"Talking? About what?"

"Just talking, Jillian," said Nan. "Please, don't do this. It's not good for you."

Jillian remained coldly inquisitorial. "Where did you go last night, Nan?"

"Please, Jillian," Nan pleaded, "listen to yourself. You're driving yourself crazy."

Jillian spoke through clenched teeth. "Just tell me. Where did you go last night?"

Nan shook her head and wiped a tear from her eye. "I love you, Jillian. Spencer loves you. We all do . . . so much . . ."

"Spencer was there, Nan," Jillian replied. "And you were the only person who could have told him about Reese."

Nan fought back her tears and looked at her sister, she bit her lip and then, reluctantly, picked up her backpack and headed for the front door of the apartment."

"I love you, Jillian," she said. "But I'm not going to do this with you . . . I love you . . ." Nan slammed the door behind her, leaving Jillian alone with that radio.

The children sang: "Itsy-Bitsy Spider." But then the song was over, and the children just sat there staring at Jillian. Her face was filled with loneliness and fear—and she was so consumed that she had not been paying attention to her class at all.

Finally a little girl summoned up the courage to speak. "Mrs. Armacost?"

Jillian shook her head as if just waking from a dream "I'm sorry, honey," she said, "what is it?"

"The song is over."

Just then the school bell rang and Jillian realized with some relief that school was over as well.

It was only a sense of duty and routine that made Jillian stop by her mailbox to see if she had missed any important announcements or handouts. There was only one piece of mail for her, an envelope which she tore open. Inside was a single piece of paper with a padlock key taped to it. Scrawled on the paper were the words: "New York Storage. Unit 345—Mrs. Armacost. Be careful." It was signed, "Sherman Reese."

Jillian rode the huge freight elevator up to the third floor of the New York Storage facility. As the giant stainless cube rose slowly, Jillian wondered what lay in store for her in Unit 345. She was about to find out.

The elevator stopped, the door opened, and Jillian stepped out. The vast storage floor, lined with hundreds of locked bins stretching off into the far shadows, was absolutely silent and poorly lit by occasional fluorescent lights. They were controlled by a large button on the wall next to the elevator. A sign above it read: TO CONSERVE ENERGY, LIGHTS SHUT OFF EVERY 30 MINUTES. Jillian did not see it; rather she was intent on finding Unit 345. The place was a maze and the only sounds were the buzz of the lights, the hum of the ventilation outlets, Jillian's footsteps on the concrete, and her breathing. She walked past row after row of white doors with numbers stenciled on them. Everything was clinical looking as if the place were a laboratory. She found door 345 and put the key in the padlock and opened it.

Jillian stepped into an eight-by-eight cube. Jillian pulled closed the door behind her and fumbled for the light switch. She snapped on the overhead and found that she was standing in the middle of a little archive. There was a desk and chair and shelves from floor to ceiling packed with folders. There were boxes of documents. Everything was neat, clean, and appeared to be organized to the point of what seemed to be mania. Part of the walls were given over to cork bulletin boards, each covered with orderly rows of newspaper clippings, all of which concerned Spencer Armacost in some way. There were sober accounts of his shuttle missions from scholarly journals, there were magazine stories that had been planted in the glossies by NASA public relations.

Sherman Reese had kept up to date. There was a picture and advertisement from *Aviation Week* showing Spencer, Nelson, and a mock-up of the McLaren jet, along with the announcement: *Coming to the skies, 2013 . . .*

Sherman Reese had been in New York for a long time before making his attempt to get in touch with her. She felt a wave of nausea when she saw the stack of photographs, all of them taken in New York City—Spencer on the sidewalk, Spencer entering the apartment building, Spencer getting into a cab . . . Spencer talking with Nan. Jillian could only wonder when that one had been taken . . .

In the middle of the desk was a videotape with a Post-it note stuck to it. It read: "For Jillian." Just as she picked it up the lights in the storage facility clicked off.

There was utter darkness for a second or two, then the dim yellow security lights kicked in. Jillian was spooked and dashed out of the storage locker, running through the maze of corridors until she found the welcoming light in front of the elevator. She punched the call button and stood in the dim light listening to her breathing, silently begging the elevator to arrive.

The elevator slid open and Jillian started to throw herself into it, but instead found herself face-to-face with a young couple pushing a large pallet piled high with storage boxes.

"Getting off," said the man.

Jillian stepped back. "Sorry," she mumbled.

They pushed their burden out on to the floor, the woman hitting the button that turned on all the lights. Trying to calm herself down, Jillian stepped into the elevator and the door closed. The panic did not sink. She was alone in the big metal box and she clutched the videotape, her arms wrapped around her belly. She was deathly afraid and she did not have the slightest idea of what.

She knew she was afraid of the videotape—but she also knew that she had to see what was on it. But Jillian steeled herself, pushed the videotape into the VCR, took the remote control, sat on the couch, and hit the play button.

There was a flash of static, then an image. Sherman Reese's hotel room. Sherman stepped in front of the camera. It was plain that he was very nervous. His laptop computer was open on the bed next to him and he glanced at it from moment to moment.

Sherman spoke directly into the camera. "It's a joke, right . . . But if you're watching this tape, then I never got to that meeting with you. If you are watching this tape, Mrs. Armacost, then I am probably fucking dead. This is the backup. That's what they always taught us at NASA," he said. "Always make sure you have a backup. This is mine . . ." He paused a moment, as if thinking about his own mortality. Then he gazed steadily into the camera lens. "I'm not crazy," Reese said. "I wish I were. I prayed I was, but I'm not." He paused again. "I've been thinking *you* might be thinking that you're crazy, too. How could you not? I mean, after all that's happened . . ."

It was as if that speech was a little prologue, an introduction to what happened next. From the pocket of his suit coat he pulled another small tape recorder, one identical to the one she had carried away from him and smashed.

It was as if Reese knew what she was thinking. He smiled crookedly. "I told you . . . always have a backup." He plugged the recorder into his laptop and hit the play button. The first voice she heard was Reese's own.

"There are two voices on the tape you are going

to hear, Mrs. Armacost. Your husband's and that of Captain Streck.''

The sonic response lines of the noise on the tape showed on the laptop screen.

Spencer spoke first: ''I'm going to rotate the main panel forty-eight degrees. You got me, Alex?''

Alex Streck's voice replied. ''That's good to go, Spencer. I'll need the 9c spanner as soon as . . . Spencer? You feel that?''

Reese pointed to his laptop screen. ''Now, you see, this line here is your husband's voice. This line here is Captain Streck's,'' he said professorially.

Spencer's voice came next. It was high and panicky. She knew it was her husband, but she had never heard him like that before. ''Alex? Jesus. *Alex*? What the—''

Reese pointed to the third line. ''Two voices but there are three lines. There's something else on this tape. Something we can't hear. Something out of our range. But . . . I translated it. I had to hear it. This is what it sounds like.''

As she listened the squalor and disappointment that had become Sherman Reese's life vanished. Instead, he was his old self, the precise, NASA-trained scientist.

Reese typed a code into the laptop, and from the speakers came that sound, the insect screaming, the horrible shrieking. The terrible noise hit Jillian like a hot bullet.

Reese killed the sound and then turned back to face the camera. ''Now, NASA said it was static.

They said it was caused by the exploding satellite.''

Jillian had reached her own conclusion. ''It's not static,'' she whispered.

''NASA said it was a static buildup in their suits,'' said Reese. ''But it's not static. I tracked it. It didn't come from the satellite. It didn't come from the suits. It didn't come from the shuttle.'' Reese's cool seemed to ebb.

''It didn't come from earth either,'' he said nervously. ''Two minutes. That's all there is. That's all it took. It's a transmission, Mrs. Armacost. If you wanted to come here, to earth, I mean, from very far away . . . maybe you wouldn't have to travel in a ship . . . maybe you could travel in a transmission. Travel at the speed of light. Like a thought. You wait for two humans to be up there . . . two of us in orbit, near a target. With something to aim at, like a satellite . . .''

Jillian was hanging on every word, staring hard at the screen. The story he was telling was so much worse than she ever imagined, she could hardly believe it.

''Two of us who are beyond suspicion,'' Reese continued. ''Heroes. All-Americans. You wait for a pair like them then . . . erase them like a tape and record your own message.''

Jillian didn't think she could hear any more. The truth was too awful to bear.

''Natalie Streck knew it,'' said Reese. ''And you know it, too, don't you? He is not your husband anymore. He's not. You know he's not.'' He looked square into the camera lens. ''Don't you?''

Reese seemed pleased that he had proven his case. He went back to his professorial mode. "That satellite they were supposed to be repairing—they weren't repairing it, they were deploying it—you know what that was for? It was designed to listen for transmissions from deep space. It was supposed to look for anything, anything coming from there at all. It was just supposed to listen." Reese laughed a little and shook his head ruefully.

"NASA thinks it failed. They think it didn't work. We know it worked. Don't we?"

Suddenly, Reese stopped talking. He appeared to listen to something beyond the view of the lens, then, without warning he jumped up, and ran from the frame. There was the sound of fumbling and static as the camera was shut down and the screen of Jillian's television set went blank. She did not move, staring at the gray snow, even though the disturbing, hair-raising "show" appeared to have come to an end.

But it hadn't ended. Abruptly the static cleared and Reese re-entered the frame. It looked as if some time had passed and Sherman looked a little worse for wear. He was holding a blueprint in his hand and he waved it at the camera.

"There's no computer to run that plane," Reese said. "It hasn't been designed yet." He unrolled the blueprint and held it close to the lens. "Once it's designed it's going to go right here, in the cockpit. Right here where the pilots should be."

Jillian moved closer to the television screen squinting at the blueprint, trying to see the point that Reese indicated with a poorly manicured fingernail.

"It's going to be a binary computer," Reese said. "Binary. That's twin, Mrs. Armacost. Twin. What do you think you have inside you? What do you think he put there?"

She couldn't take any more. She turned off the VCR and leaned back on the sofa, her head reeling. She could see herself in the bathtub, Spencer kneeling next to her, washing her, attending to her. She heard Spencer's voice. "What will they be? Pilots?"

Jillian lay on the couch, the television remote control in one hand and remembered well what she had said that night. "Pilots . . . just like their father." She sat there still for a moment, the silence in the apartment was overwhelming. It made Spencer's voice sound that much louder.

"Jillian?"

She jumped and dropped the VCR remote as she turned to face her husband. "I didn't hear you come in," she said, doing her best to recover from her obvious surprise. "You're home early."

Spencer sat down next to her on the couch. Jillian watched anxiously as Spencer toyed absently with the VCR remote control. He tossed it lightly from hand to hand.

"I felt bad for you, getting into that fight with Nan."

"How do you know about that?"

"She called."

"And she didn't tell you what it was about?"

Spencer shook his head. "She said, 'None of your business, Spaceman.' "

"That's right," Jillian answered. "It was just sister stuff. She'll get over it and so will I."

Spencer ran his thumb up the remote, his finger playing on the play button.

"You haven't heard from her?"

Jillian shook her head and watched his fingers play around the buttons.

"Well," said Spencer, "I wouldn't worry . . . I'm sure she'll call soon enough."

Jillian could not stand it any longer. She reached out and placed her hand on her husband's. He stopped fiddling with the buttons. He touched her fingers.

"Jillian, you are trembling."

"Am I?" Jillian said as lightly as she could. "I guess I'm just a little cold."

Spencer put his arms around her as if to warm her. "I have something here to cheer you up."

Spencer reached into his briefcase and pulled out a videocassette and waved it at her.

"*Follow the Fleet*," he said. "Fred, Ginger, me, you. What do you say? How about it?"

Spencer went to the VCR and tried to load the tape, but he found the bay occupied. "You watching something?" he asked, looking over his shoulder at her.

He popped out the tape of Sherman Reese's expose. "No label," he said. There was the faintest sound of suspicion in his voice. "What is this thing?"

The lie came so easily, Jillian was astonished by herself. "It's a pregnancy video," she said. "Denise gave it to me. She thought it would make me feel better."

Spencer loaded *Follow the Fleet*. The he joined her on the couch, taking her in his arms. "You worry too much, Jilly." He hit the play button and they waited while the feeder tape spooled through the VCR.

"Why are you building that plane?" Jillian asked, trying to keep her voice light and casual.

Spencer laughed. "What? What are you talking about, Jillian? I don't get it."

"That plane . . . that terrible plane that you and Jackson and McLaren are so proud of . . . Why do you have to build it? Why does it have to exist at all?"

Spencer shrugged. "It's a contract, Jilly. And I didn't add as much as Jackson said I did . . . They have a bunch of real smart engineers over there. They're behind most of it."

The first notes of *Follow the Fleet* began to flow from the VCR, but neither of them were paying attention.

"I know what you're thinking," said Spencer. "You're worried about what kind of world we'll be bringing the twins into. I think about it, too, believe me . . ."

They settled down to watch the movie. "Don't worry," he said reassuringly. "We won't let anything happen to them. Will we? I know you won't and you know I won't.

Follow the Fleet played on the television, but it played to no conscious audience. Both Jillian and Spencer had fallen asleep, entwined in each other's arms.

Jillian dreamed. A dream so real that even in her sleep she hated it. Those familiar words.

"I'm going to rotate the panel forty-eight degrees. You got me, Alex?"

"That's good to go. I'll need the 9c spanner as soon as . . . Spencer? You feel that?"

"Alex? Jesus. *Alex*? What the—"

Jillian awoke with a start, waking Spencer at the same time. *Follow the Fleet* was still on the television set.

Spencer pulled Jillian into an embrace. "Must have dozed off," he said.

"Were you dreaming?" Jillian asked.

"No," said Spencer, "just sleeping."

"You weren't dreaming?" Jillian pressed.

"No, Jillian. I wasn't dreaming," he said.

Jillian looked into his eyes. They were not loving, but black and cold.

"Were you?" Spencer asked.

Jillian looked down at the coffee table where Sherman Reese's video cassette had been before they fell asleep. The tape was gone. Jillian felt her stomach lurch.

"Were you?" Spencer repeated.

Jillian looked over at the radio and closed her eyes. "No," she said. "No dreams for me."

18

There were any number of restaurants on Madison Avenue that catered to the rich women who constituted the New York corps known as "The Ladies who Lunch." Shelley McLaren was known at all of them, but she favored one of them above all others. She was sure to get the best table no matter how late she called for a reservation, she was always welcome to order "off the menu"—asking for things not listed on the menu, that is—and for these privileges she was mercilessly overcharged, but because she was one of the few who had a house charge at the restaurant she had no idea how much money she actually paid for her microscopic lunches or how astronomically she tipped.

Not that she would have cared all that much, but like all rich people she did not like being taken advantage of. Nevertheless, when Jillian Armacost called with a special request, Shelley had insisted that she treat to lunch at "her" place at Madison and Seventy-seventh. Jillian was on time and shown to the table immediately. Shelley walked through the door fewer than three minutes later, but it took her a full thirty minutes to make it to the table.

Finally she plunked herself down in front of Jillian. "Sorry about that," she said. "One knows so many people in places like this and you have to chitchat with all of them or the next thing you know they won't support your charity and your tickets to the Costume Institute Reception at the Metropolitan suddenly go to some woman from Minneapolis that you've never heard of . . ."

"I never knew lunch could be so complicated," said Jillian. "What if you just stayed home and had a sandwich?"

"Social death," said Shelly McLaren. She popped open her Judith Lieber purse and worked around in there for a moment. "Lunch may be complicated," she said as she searched. "But strangely enough the most complicated things can be surprisingly simple." She pulled a brown plastic vial filled with prescription pills from her purse and showed them to Jillian, passing them quickly across the table as a waiter glided up to them, smiling unctuously.

"Good afternoon, Mrs. McLaren," he said. "It is so nice to see you again."

"Two glasses of muscadet, Charlie," Shelly ordered. "Two of those nice salads and leave us alone."

"Very good, ma'am." Charlie withdrew quickly.

Shelley leaned forward and smiled at Jillian. Jillian was fingering the pill bottle under the table.

"Now, about these things," said Shelley. "My caterer gets them from someone in the French Caribbean. Martinique, I think. The French are so advanced in this sort of thing, don't you think? RU486 was supposed to have been legal here years ago, but it will never happen . . ."

The waiter named Charlie returned with the wine and Shelley clammed up as he placed the glasses in front of them. They waited a couple of seconds before speaking again.

"Are they safe?" Jillian asked.

"Yes," Shelley replied. "But there's really something you should know before you—" She was silent again as the salads were delivered and Charlie withdrew.

"What should I know?" Jillian asked. This was not a meeting she had relished, but she has thought about it hard and long and now she was determined to go through with it.

"With these things, Jillian," said Shelley, "all sales are final. You take them and you'll abort. You have to ask yourself, do you want to go through with this?"

Jillian nodded. "Yes. Absolutely."

"Okay," said Shelley. "Take both pills when you get home. Then go lie down for a while. Then there will be quite a bit of vile cramping, then once you start spotting it goes pretty fast." Shelley took a slug of her wine. "Believe me, if I can get through it, anyone can."

"You?" said Jillian.

Shelley had to stop herself from rolling her eyes.

"Jillian, we all have. It's like there's a secret club. There's 'the Pill' and then, just in case, there's 'the Pills.'"

"And Spencer won't know?"

Shelley picked up her wine glass again and waved off an imaginary Spencer. "If he's anything like the rest of them . . . he'll think it was a miscarriage and fly down to Van Cleef's to buy you a bracelet. If he feels really bad he'd go to Harry Winston's." Shelley extended her wrist and rattled a thick diamond bracelet on her wrist.

"Unless he's looking for it," Shelley continued, "there will be no way to tell. And why should he be looking for it?"

Neither of them had touched their salads and Jillian had not had her wine, but Shelley signaled for the check. Charlie brought it and Shelley signed it. The she looked over at Jillian who appeared to be on the verge of tears.

Shelley put her hand on Jillian's. "Don't beat yourself up about this, sweetheart," she said. "It's not as if any of this means anything, you know. It's all nonsense . . ."

Jillian stood in the bright white of the bathroom connected to her bedroom and looked at the bottle of pills. Very slowly she unscrewed the top and shook the contents into her hand. The two tablets were very thick and dusty. They would be difficult to force down her dry throat. She ran the water in the sink and filled a glass with it—she was about to put the pills in her mouth when she began to hear her own heart beating, getting louder and louder until she could hear nothing else. But then there came another sound . . . a much faster thump. Two more heartbeats. The heart beats of the twin fetuses, pounding away so fast as if telegraphing a message to their mother, begging not to be killed.

"Please . . ." Jillian whimpered. "Please."

She looked down at the pills in her palm and her hand trembled. The fast beating of the fetuses' hearts seemed to grown in volume and intensity. Jillian became even more fearful.

"Be quiet," she begged. "Be quiet, please . . . He'll hear you. He'll come in here." She had no idea where Spencer was, but she had become convinced that there was some kind of psychic bond between the things in her belly and the man masquerading as her husband.

But the twin hearts only beat louder and faster, and added to the disconcerting noise was the whoosh and whine of the amniotic fluid that surrounded and protected them.

The pills were still in her hand and the glass of water was poised. Jillian was crying, fat tears rolling down her cheeks. "Please, I have to . . . It's okay, it's okay . . . it'll be over soon . . . please . . ."

But it wouldn't be. The moment she spoke those words a terrible pain ripped through her body—it seemed to scorch her belly—driving her to her knees. She clutched the pills so tightly in her fist that they might have been ground to powder.

From her knees Jillian gasped, "I'm sorry . . . I have to. It'll be better this way. It will be, I promise.'' She opened her hands and looked down at the pills.

"I can't,'' she cried. "Oh God, I can't do it . . .''

Behind her the bathroom door flew open and Spencer charged into the room.

"What were you going to do to them?''

When Jillian turned and saw him, she screamed and forced herself to her feet.

"What are those pills? What were you going to do with them?''

"Oh God, you heard them,'' Jillian cried, "didn't you? They called out to you.''

Spencer forced calm into his voice and tried to take her in his arms. "Jillian . . .''

"Oh Jesus, you heard them,'' she wailed. She backed away from him then ran from the bathroom and through the bedroom. Spencer chased after her.

"Jillian, it's okay,'' he shouted. "Really. It's okay, Jillian, please stop.''

She was headed for the front door—no idea in her head where she might be going except that she knew she had to get away from him—but when she reached it Spencer stood there, barring her flight.

He put out his hands for her and moved slowly towards her. "Jilly, please,'' he said soothingly. "It is going to be all right. You have to try and calm down. That's all.''

But Jillian wasn't buying it. She backed away from him, shaking her head, desperate to think of what she might do next.

"Jillian,'' said Spencer. Then he reached for her as another spasm of that horrible pain ripped through her. She doubled over and fell hard, tumbling down the steps, hitting the bottom with sickening force. But she managed to stagger to her feet, a dazed and dreamy look on her face as she looked up the stairs at Spencer.

"Jillian, please . . ." Then he got a very strange look on his face. And even in her dazed and pain-wracked state she noticed it.

"Spencer? What is it?"

Jillian followed the line of his gaze and saw that he was staring at the patch between her legs. The material of her clothing was sodden with blood and a long line of gore had trickled down her leg.

She said, "Spencer?" She saw him coming down the stairs toward her, but she saw him as if in stop-motion, each blink an exposure bringing him a little closer. Then everything went black. And silent.

Then everything was noise and bright lights. Jillian had no idea how much time had passed, but she knew she was in a hospital. She could tell by the sound and the smells and the speed of the rolling gurney. There were doctors and nurses surrounding the moving bed, looking down *at* her, talking *about* her. But no one was talking *to* her.

"You must keep him away from me," she managed to say. Those few words seem to exhaust her and she felt that terrible weakness of the helpless.

"She's still hemorrhaging," a nurse announced.

"Please," Jillian gasped. "Please . . . please . . ."

A doctor spoke, his tone matter-of-fact and dispassionate. "If she's still hemorrhaging then she's going to bleed out in a minute or two. Pure and simple."

Jillian thought she heard herself saying "Please . . . please . . ." But she couldn't be sure if she was saying the words or merely thinking them. She tried to raise her hand to her lips but she could not find them. She did not know if she had been sedated or if she was dying. She heard someone say, "Is there an O.R. free?"

Jillian was looking up as a surgical team prepared itself. There were lots of doctors and nurses in those scary green-colored scrubs. Bright lights were shone into her eyes. There seemed to be tons of equipment—monitors, lights, shiny tanks of oxygen and anesthetics. There was lots of noise and clatter.

All faces were obscured by surgical masks; all she could see were their eyes. And there was only one set of eyes she recognized in all of them. Spencer's.

"Please . . ." she said. But no one paid any attention to her, the woman they were about to save.

19

Jillian had no idea how much time had passed. She knew she was in a hospital, she was sure of that if nothing else, and as she faded from consciousness to unconsciousness she saw faces she knew—Nan, Shelley McLaren and Spencer, always Spencer, hovering over her bed, his eyes fixed on hers, watching her, evaluating her the way a farmer looks over his brood stock.

A variety of doctors attended her—she didn't know one of them—and they poked and prodded her, and thrust needles into her arms, then retired to corners to discuss her as if she was not there lying in her bed in her darkened room.

She heard them say things like, "Psychiatric . . . evaluations . . . her husband's care . . ."

Jillian heard Spencer's voice and felt him take her hand. "The twins are fine," he said soothingly. "They are still inside you, safe and sound, right where they should be. We are never going to mention what you tried to do . . . with those pills. It's over now. It's behind us. It didn't happen, did it, Jilly?''

She wanted to tell him that there had been a reason for those pills. That she was doing the right thing . . . But her voice . . . it just would not work. ''Spencer . . .''

''I'm here,'' he said. ''Don't try to talk. I love you so much, you know that? You scared me. If anything had happened, I could not have gone on without with you. We have to be together, Jillian, you, me, the babies . . . we're all one now.''

Jillian thrashed in the bed, but she could hardly move. She was tethered by a thicket of intravenous tubes. ''No . . .'' she said. ''Spencer . . .''

''Sssshhh,'' said Spencer, as if talking to a child. ''Don't try to talk, Jillian. Don't even try.''

The first thing she noticed was that she was enveloped in a cloud of Chanel Number Five, and then she felt some lips on her cheek. And then Shelley McLaren's voice in her ear.

''I am so sorry, sweetheart.''

Jillian knew exactly what she was talking about. For some reason, that lunch came back vividly, she remembered every detail, from the muscadet to the uneaten salads. . . . the waiter's name had been Charlie, she recalled. And she had not forgotten that the luncheon had been arranged to arrange a pair of abortions.

''I couldn't do it . . .'' Jillian told Shelley. ''They are part of me. I can feel them in there. The blood that runs through my heart runs through their hearts. I couldn't do it . . .''

Shelley bent down and smiled at her. "If I had known . . . if I had known about your past I would never have given you those pills to you . . . never . . ." Shelley leaned down a bit more and kissed her cheek. "Let me open the shades in here, you need a little light in here, I think. Don't you, darling?"

Shelley left the bed and pulled on the cords and the blinds opened and the room was flooded with light.

"They are mine," said Jillian. "Not his. I want to keep them safe. I have to keep them safe."

The sunlight was blinding and Jillian could only make out the vague edges of Shelley McLaren's body. "Shelley," Jillian asked, "who told you about my past?"

There was no answer.

Seconds later, the blinds swept back and the room fell into darkness again. Jillian raised her head again from the bed and saw Spencer at the window.

She could not be sure if Shelley McLaren had ever been there. She could still smell the Chanel Number Five. But she had no idea what that meant.

Jillian smiled when she heard Denise's voice. "You gave us a real scare, Jillian," she said.

"How long have I been here?" Jillian's voice was cracked and doped up.

"You have been unconscious for nearly two weeks," Denise replied. She was staring at Jillian's voluminous chart as she spoke. "Your bleeding was awful. You hemorrhaged quite severely. You lost a great deal of blood."

Jillian tried to sit up, but Denise gently pushed her back down on the mattress. "You *have* to remain calm now, Jillian," Denise said solemnly. "One of the miracles of pregnancy is that your body took care of the babies, even putting their welfare ahead of its own needs. All through this, they got plenty of blood and more than enough nutrition. But I am prescribing bed rest for the term of your pregnancy. Your husband has arranged for a home nurse when you get out. You'll be having complete, around the clock care."

Deftly, Denise inserted a hypodermic needle into one of the shunts in Jillian's IV tube and shot a dose of sedative into it.

"Rest is the most important thing now," said Denise. "You have to believe me . . ."

Then there was Nan. She appeared . . . one morning? Evening? Jillian had no idea. But she was there, standing over her bed with tears in her eyes, looking at her as if Jillian was some kind of basket case. Nonetheless, Jillian was very glad to see her sister. She smiled though her cracked and dry lips and said her name.

"Nanny . . ." The word came out slurred, but there was no doubting the happiness behind it.

"Oh, Jilly . . ." Nan snatched one of her hands. "I didn't want to fight you, Jilly . . . I didn't want to."

As Nan leaned down to hug her sister, Jillian whispered in her ear. "Something's wrong, Nan."

Nan shook her head. "No, there's nothing wrong. The doctors say you can go home any day now. Everything is going to be okay from now on."

Jillian's heart sank. Nan was another one who wouldn't listen, or who was determined not to understand. Maybe she didn't want to understand. "There's something horrible, Nan. With Spencer. And with the twins, too."

"No, Jilly," said Nan. "It's nothing but this place. It will all look different when you're out of here."

But Jillian would not be dissuaded. She was determined that somebody understand what had happened to her. "He did something to me," Jillian said. "Something horrible. I should have told you about it before."

"No, no," said Nan, shaking her head. "You're just all messed up because you've been in the hospital for so long. That's what makes you feel like this ... I know you must hate it here. I know I would. We're going to take you home soon. We're all going to take care of you. We'll take good care of you, Jilly-o."

Jillian felt a familiar feeling fear. "All of you? Does that mean Spencer, too?"

Nan smiled. "Of course, Jilly."

"And you, too?"

"Yes, Jilly," said Nan. "All of us."

"And Shelley McLaren? What about Shelley?"

Jillian watched as a look of sadness sweep across

Nan's face. Nan shrugged and opened her mouth to say something, but did not answer Jillian's question.

But Jillian understood. "She's dead, isn't she?

Nan would not look at her sister. "Now why would you say a thing like that."

Jillian shook her head, unhappy that her sister would not tell her the truth. "Something is wrong."

"Why would you say that?" Nan asked.

"Something is wrong . . . something is wrong with Spencer. Something is wrong with the twins. Something is wrong with the whole thing."

Nan seemed a little overeager in her questions. "Okay, what's wrong? Tell me, Jilly, what? What?"

"He's hiding, Nan . . . he's hiding inside."

Jillian felt herself sinking slowly into unconsciousness. From far away she heard Nan's voice. "What do you mean, Jilly, hiding inside? What does that mean . . . ?"

But Jillian was gone . . .

When she awoke the next time it was raining hard, the raindrops rattling against the windows like handfuls of gravel. It was a sad, dispiriting sound. Standing at the window, watching the rain, was Spencer. Jillian felt her heart sink when she saw him, but she had to speak to him.

"I saw Reese," she croaked. "I saw you and Sherman Reese, you were together."

Spencer's laugh was obviously forced. "Sherman Reese? I saw him, too. He's crazy, Jillian. Obsessed. You can't let thoughts like that in your head. You have to be strong, Jillian. For the babies. For us. And most of all, for yourself . . .''

Jillian was not going to be put off by his continual platitudes. It was always them, me, us, you . . . "But Reese . . ." Jillian said. "Reese said that . . ."

Spencer marched from the window and leaned down close to her. "Jillian . . . If the doctors knew what you were thinking . . . those kinds of dark thoughts. What do you think they would do? They know about your past . . . They are concerned about you, about the babies, about your health, your well-being. If they thought you were going off the rails about Sherman Reese, tell me, Jillian . . . do you think you would ever get out of this hospital?''

As if to belie his threat, Spencer kissed her softly and slowly.

She hated his touch.

In a walk-in closet in Jillian and Spencer's apartment, Spencer studied every piece of paper that Sherman Reese had managed to cram into his already overstuffed briefcase. He was amazed at how the man had managed to take a few facts and spin them into a scenario that was dangerously close to the the whole truth.

Nan found Spencer entranced by the document and the tapes. She had no idea what he was looking at, it meant nothing to her. She was more interested in the welfare of her sister.

"Spencer, are you going to the hospital?" she

asked. "I am. She's got so much on her mind . . . some of it doesn't make sense, but it's pretty intense."

Spencer continued to study the documents. "What do you mean?" he asked.

"She's pretty pissed at you, for one thing," said Nan. "She thinks you're out to get her."

"She's wrong," said Spencer. He still did not look up from the papers.

Nan peered over his shoulder. "What's so interesting there? What are you reading?"

Spencer stood up and grabbed Nan by the wrist. Immediately she tried to pull away. "Let go of me," she said.

But Spencer pulled her close. It was gentle. He did not have to threaten her with physical pain. "I said, let go of me." With her free hand Nan raked her nails along his forearm, pulling away skin and drawing bright blood. He winced in pain but did not let go of her. Instead he drew Nan close, like a lover. Spencer bent at the waist and put his mouth to her ear, whispering something. Immediately, Nan began to scream in pain, desperately trying to claw at her own ears to keep his voice from her hearing. But her hands were pinned. He would not let her go and continued to speak to her.

Then Nan stopped screaming. Blood broke from her lips and her eyes went blank.

Very slowly, Spencer allowed her broken dead body to slip to the floor of the closet, her blood flooding out on to the dog-eared papers and documents that had once been the property of the hapless, now deceased, Sherman Reese.

As Nan hit the floor, Jillian, in her hospital bed felt . . . something, something that wakened her. Something grim and awful. She felt as if a part of her had been killed and she sat bolt upright in the bed and screamed. *"Nan!"*

20

Jillian was determined to get out of the bed. She *had* to get out of that damn hospital. It took her a while to remove all of the IV tubes from her arm. Then she pushed down the gate on the right side of the bed, swung herself around, and sat there for a moment, her feet poised above the cold hospital floor. Then she pushed herself off, as if launching herself into the void, her toes making contact with the floor. She held herself steady against the bed for a moment or two, then straightened and staggered toward the closet on the far side of the room. She was going to get dressed and get out of there.

There were clothes, fresh, clean clothes, in that closet, clothes that Nan had placed there, put away like a bride's trousseau, against some happy day in the future. It took a while for her to get dressed— she had never realized what complicated things zippers could be, and how recalcitrant and difficult buttons are, but she managed to get herself dressed and out of the hospital room without being detected.

It was still very early in the morning and Jillian could totter down the hallway undetected. All around her the sick and the insane were sleeping. The nurses were not at their posts and most of the doctors had left the building. Jillian carefully made her way to the elevator bank at the end of the corridor.

Mercifully, the elevator was empty and with a sudden burst of happiness, she stepped into the car. Her happiness did not last long. As the elevator reached the ground floor and the double metal doors swept open Jillian found herself looking out at another hospital corridor and two exhausted-looking interns standing there waiting for a ride.

Jillian trembled with fear.

''Ma'am?'' said one of the doctors in training. ''Ma'am? Are you okay?'' She saw the two young men and the hospital hallway behind them, but beyond, the corridor raced off into the blackness of space. This time the stars were gone.

''Are you okay?'' he repeated.

Jillian managed to nod and she stepped off the elevator walking with the exaggerated precision of a drunk. The two interns looked at her, then at each other, and shrugged. They were really too tired to care . . .

Outside of the hospital the world appeared to be normal. She walked down the sidewalk, looking for a cab, but there was none in sight. Up ahead was a bus shelter, glowing in the dark from the light of its advertising panel. She walked to it and stopped there a moment, hoping for a bus, then realizing she knew nothing about the New York City bus system. As soon as she decided she would wait there and throw herself on the mercy of the driver of the first bus to come along, she saw something that made her wince with terror. A man was coming down the street, walking fast and purposefully. She had no idea who he was, but she had no doubt that he was coming for her.

Jillian ran, dashed a round a corner, and almost ran into a cab that was just pulling away from the curb, having just dropped a fare. Frantically she waved it down and threw herself into the back seat. The driver could not be seen, hidden as he was behind dark and scratched Plexiglas. She leaned forward and blurted out her address.

"Yes, missus, very good," the driver replied to her instructions. He had a heavy foreign accent and that reassured her. There was no way it could be Spencer.

Jillian sat back in the seat and looked out at the passing cityscape. Everything appeared as it should. There were a couple of people on the sidewalk, there were cars on the street. She allowed herself to relax for a moment—until the cab rolled to a stop for a red light at an intersection. Jillian felt the fear again and she looked through the back window to see another cab a few hundred yards behind bearing down on her. Jillian pounded on the Plexiglas.

"Go! Go!" she screamed at the driver.

"But it is red, missus," came the reply.

Jillian was crying now. "Go, please, please go . . ."

"But, missus, I cannot."

"Oh God," she gasped. She had to get out of that cab. She grabbed the handle and threw open the door. But New York City had vanished, replaced by the vast blackness of space. Jillian slammed the door and fell back on the cracked vinyl of the seats panting and sobbing, so filled with terror she was paralyzed.

Then from the front seat she heard Spencer's voice, calm and reasonable.

"You see it too, don't you?" Spencer said softly. "Don't you, Jillian?"

"Yes," she gasped, her voice broken and hoarse.

"And it's just us, all alone . . . no one else knows," said Spencer.

Jillian nodded. "Yes," she said.

"Just us . . . and now you know."

"It's not a dream," Jillian whispered. She opened the car door and stepped out into the street and ran. But Spencer's voice followed her, she could hear it in her head, she could hear it all around her, as if he had taken over the city.

"Look around," he said. "These people don't know you. No one knows you. Only me. It's just us now, Jillian. You and me. And what's inside you . . . we're connected."

But even as she heard her husband's voice she heard the voice of the cab driver, irate and screaming about her running out on her fare . . .

*   *   *

The subway train screamed into the station like a demon, its iron wheels shrieking on the track as it came to a stop. The doors swept open and Jillian entered and sat on a bench. There were a few tired-looking night workers in the car, wending their way home after a long, dark shift in the office towers of the city. No one looked at Jillian and she made no eye contact. She gazed out the window, but as the kinescopic flash of light and dark in the subway tunnel danced before her eyes, a series of random images thrust themselves into her brain. She saw herself in bed with Spencer, *Follow the Fleet* on TV, Fred Astaire singing.

Fred Astaire's voice died away and she saw another scene from her life. Jillian and Spencer were in bed again. But this time they were in their bed in New York. Jillian was flat on her back as if drugged, Spencer on top of her, thrusting into her. Somewhere nearby was the insect sound . . .

Jillian burst into tears, and an old woman across the aisle looked at her. The scream of the subway wheels masked the sounds of her sobs.

Now she was on the examination table in Denise's office. On the ultrasound monitor she could see the twins, in utero, more fully formed than she had ever seen them. Their eyes stared out, their mouths open as they floated inside of her.

The twins vanished, replaced by the horrific scene of Natalie Streck standing over that bathroom sink. Jillian could see herself in that mirror, and behind her stood Spencer.

The subway shrieked as it pulled into a station.

The doors creaked open and Jillian jumped to her feet and fled.

It was so quiet and so still on the street. She was nearly at her apartment building and she was alone. She put one hand on her stomach and wept with relief. Then she heard a whisper behind her.

Spencer said, "Jillian?" His voice sounded heavy with relief. Jillian whipped around and saw him walking quickly toward her. She screamed and ran for the front door of her building.

"Jillian!" Spencer shouted. "Please . . ."

But she didn't stop. She burst into the foyer of her building, her sudden appearance waking the snoozing night doorman. He sat up behind the desk and blinked at her as she ran for the elevator. She hit the up button hard.

"Everything okay there, Mrs. A?" the night man asked.

The elevator was a long time coming. Jillian looked at the street door, then back at the elevator, willing it to come.

"Hey, look," said the doorman. "Here comes your husband, Mrs. A."

Jillian did not answer. The elevator arrived and she jumped into it and vanished. The doorman shrugged. Lovers' tiff, he figured. He'd seen it a million times before.

Jillian threw open the door of the apartment and locked the door behind her. She put all her weight behind the bench next to the door and dragged it a few feet to barricade the entrance.

A few seconds later the front door opened and thumped against the heavy bench. "Jillian?" Spencer called through the narrow gap. "Jillian, what are you doing?" He threw his weight against the door and the bench moved a few inches.

Jillian knew she had very little time. She ran to the living room and pulled the plug on the radio and then raced to the kitchen and turned on both taps in the sink, water gushing against the basin and slopping onto the floor.

The front door flew open and Spencer stood there, stock-still, listening to the sound of water running. It seemed to be gushing all over the apartment.

"Jillian?" he yelled.

But Jillian did not answer . . .

He found her in the kitchen. She was sitting on a stool, an island in the middle of a flooded room. She was barefoot and in one hand she held one end of an extension cord; the other end was plugged into a wall socket. The radio was on the flooded counter, soaked with water. All she had to do was plug the extension cord into the radio and the entire pool in the kitchen would become electrified. She planted her bare feet in the water and looked at her husband defiantly.

"Stay away from us," Jillian growled, her voice low and feral. As Spencer watched she brought the two contacts close together, the two points almost touching.

"Jillian, please . . ." Spencer pleaded.

"Who are you?" she demanded.

"For God's sake, Jillian . . ." Spencer would not give an inch in this battle of nerves.

"What did you do to me?" Jillian demanded angrily. "What have you done?"

Spencer's voice dropped to a pleading whisper. "Jillian, please . . . just take your feet out of the water."

Jillian looked down at her feet and shook her head. "No," she said.

Spencer advanced a step. "Jillian . . . let me help you. It doesn't have to be like this."

Jillian's voice was soft but determined. "No . . . it doesn't." She looked at him squarely. "Who are you?"

"I love you, Jilly."

She shook her head. She was not going to fall for that. "No," she said. "Tell me who you are."

"I'm your husband," said Spencer simply.

"No!" Jillian yelled. "No you're not!"

"I know the first time I saw you, you were under that tree, laughing with your friends."

The memory was correct, but it had been remembered by the wrong person. "That wasn't you."

The water was still streaming onto the counter, swamping the radio and pouring on to the floor. The water was washing up against Spencer's shoes. He took a step back.

"Remember what you said to me, the first time we kissed?"

"That wasn't you."

Spencer pushed on. "You laughed and you said

'What am I going to do with you?' Do you remember that, Jillian?''

"That wasn't you," she snapped. "That was Spencer."

" 'What am I going to do with you?' And we talked, all the time, about our lives, our future . . . our family . . . Remember how I held you, when it was dark, when you were in that . . . that place. Remember? I held you, Jill, so tight." That place was the hospital where she had been confined when her parents had been killed.

"That was Spencer."

"Please, Jillian, take your feet out of the water."

Jillian did not. But she tried to be calm nonetheless. "The plane . . . That signal it's going to send . . . What happened to Spencer, up there. It's going to happen to all of us, isn't it. To all of us. You're just the first, just the first . . ."

"Jillian . . ."

Jillian held her stomach. "They will never fly it. I won't let them and you can't make them."

"You know you can't hurt them, Jillian. You know you love them, we both do."

As Spencer spoke, his gaze dropped from Jillian's face until he was looking at her belly.

Jillian grabbed herself tighter. "Leave them alone!" she ordered. Then, more calmly, quieter: "Leave them alone . . ."

Jillian rubbed the two points together. Suddenly the roar of running water mixed with the very faint sound of babies crying.

"I saved you once, Jillian," he said. "Remember

that? Please let me do it again." He held out his hands. "Please come here."

"That was Spencer," she said. Her voice was filled with steel. "Spencer is dead." Suddenly it was full of hate. "Spencer is dead and you killed him."

Spencer was in agony. He knew that if he could get near her, he could overpower her, but the threatening tide of water was right at his feet. Once again he was forced to take a step back.

"Jillian, come here," he said, throwing out his arms to her. The action pulled back the sleeve of his shirt and she saw the scratch marks that Nan had carved in his forearms.

Instantly Jillian knew the source. "Oh, my God," she wailed. "You killed her."

Spencer looked down at the scratches, then over at Jillian. There was a new and strange tone in his voice as he spoke to her this time. "Listen to them, Jillian."

"Oh God," Jillian cried out.

"Let them teach you what to see. Let them show you. They have already started."

"No. *No!*" Jillian could not tolerate the thought that the children in her womb might be evil.

"Now, Jillian," Spencer commanded. "Come here. Now!"

"Never," Jillian whispered.

They were at a standoff. Husband and wife just stared at each other, neither willing to give an inch. The only sound was the rushing water.

Frustration and fury were beginning to build in Spencer. His jaw clenched tight like a trap, his fists opened and closed. He started to pant like an animal as he stared at her with the intensity of lasers. The stool upon which Jillian was sitting began to tremble, then to shake, and then it started to move. First an inch, then another. To her horror she realized that she was being drawn toward Spencer. He was dragging her to him by sheer force of will. Jillian's eyes were wide with terror.

"Open up to them, Jillian. Let them in. Let us in. Can't you feel us?"

She was being drawn closer and he reached out, but she was still beyond his grasp. She stared at him hard, her eyes burning with hate.

"Let them, Jillian, let them bring you here. We belong together, all of us."

The tears coursed down her cheeks as she was drawn inexorably closer.

"That's good," said Spencer. "That's good, Jillian."

"Why did you come here?" Her voice was a heartbreaking wail of despair. "Why us?" Then she saw that the water had worked its way around Spencer, touching his heels.

"You will never get them," she said.

Spencer smiled. "They are already mine."

"What do you see?" asked Jillian.

Spencer looked puzzled. She pointed to the radio. "How do you get it to make sound? I turn it on and all I get is music." Spencer was surrounded by water now and he lunged for her.

"All I get is music," she said as she pulled her feet from the water and perched them on the wooden stool. Then she pushed the radio plug into the extension cord.

Spencer had time to say "Jillian, no!" before the electricity hit. The room seemed to come alive, humming with energy, the relentless sound of electric current. It was as if an electrical storm had erupted in the middle of the apartment.

Spencer was standing rigid, his body trembling. Bloody tears began to ooze from his eyes. He forced open his mouth and from it came not words, but that horrible sound, the screaming of insects. All over the apartment lightbulbs began to explode, the sparks streaking around the space like lightning. Blood was dripping from each of Spencer's ten rigid fingers. For a moment there was darkness all around except for an ethereal light that illuminated their two faces, as if they were in space. The only sound was the screech issuing from Spencer's twisted and contorted mouth.

Then, with a flash of bright light, the room lit up again and Spencer dropped to his knees in the deadly water. Then he fell, bleeding and prostrate at-Jillian's feet. Abruptly, the screaming stopped.

And all was silent for what seemed like an unnaturally long span of seconds. Then without warning, Spencer's body twitched, as if his corpse were giving in to a final death spasm. As she looked at him, she realized, to her horror, that this was not the involuntary shudder of a dead man. Rather, it was a shrug, a shake of his entire body as if he were somehow throwing off the mantle of his horrible death.

Then, before Jillian's terrified gaze, Spencer's body seemed to open and something, some *thing*, rose out of the corpse, as if an evil soul were vacating a useless cadaver.

Suddenly, the insect-like screaming began again, louder then ever. The twin fetuses inside of her kicked an abrupt and violent tattoo against the wall of her womb as if welcoming the hideous apparition and betraying her at the same time.

The thing was light and dark and without corporeal form. She sensed the thing rather than actually saw it—and what she sensed chilled her to the depths of her soul. She could feel the presence of absolute evil in that cold wet room and it emanated from that thing like the heat given off by a roaring bonfire.

Then the entire room went berserk. Every appliance in the kitchen turned on—flames erupted from the burners on the stove, sending jets of fire halfway to the ceiling, the microwave seemed to scream, the dishwasher churned as if it contained a hurricane, and the refrigerator door flew open and vomited forth its contents. Food flew in every direction and ice cubes ricocheted like cold bullets, snapping and cracking on the tiled walls.

And the radio turned on, the dial running crazily up through all the bands, trailing a mad scrabble of speech and snatches of music, and then it shot back down again and stopped at its special place. The speaker erupted with the screeching, the scream of the alien.

The thing itself was everywhere in the room and

it was nowhere as well. It danced around the chaotic kitchen, darting to the ceiling, then plummeting to the wet floor. But no matter where it was, she could feel it drawing ever closer to her, as if it were attempting to dominate her, to overcome her resolve.

Then suddenly and without warning, it was on her, pressed against her with unimaginable force, stuck to her like a second layer of skin. She could feel it trying to physically enter her, trying to burrow in and possess her, both body and soul.

In an instant all of her nerves were alive and tingling, all of her defenses were up. Her muscles tensed until they were as tight as steel cables and her jaw clenched until her teeth cracked. She summoned up every ounce of strength she possessed, every last iota of will in her mind to fight the power that bore down on her so relentlessly.

But Jillian found herself fighting a battle on two fronts. She struggled against the power outside of herself while her twin babies seemed to gnaw at her from within, as they were urging her to surrender herself to the power so much greater then she.

"No, no, *no*!" She said through clenched teeth. "I cannot let this happen." She may have been talking to her unborn children, she may have been trying to convince herself.

Then there was nothing.

It was as if in response to her words, but the struggle abruptly stopped. The force backed off, pulling away from her. She could feel it go. Deep down inside of her body, the twins fell silent and still. She was trembling with the effort she had expended.

Jillian used that moment of quiet to draw a single, deep calming breath. For a split second she allowed herself to relax . . .

Then out of nowhere, it struck, hitting her with the force of a wrenching body blow, overwhelming her weakened defenses. She could feel the power of the alien pouring into her, as if it were water rushing through a break in a dam. Suddenly, she felt as if she were drowning in the slimy spirit of this foreign, unnatural thing. She could feel it deep inside of her. It was corroding her soul like acid.

Terror seized her as she realized that she had come face to face with the end of her own life. She opened her mouth to scream at the horror of it all, but the sound caught in her throat, as if ensnared in a terrible trap.

Jillian's eyes opened wide and the pupils seemed to glow crazily for a moment. Then her face—her eyes—shut down, closing flat and dead. The last of the evil had entered through her eyes and then shut off the light of life that had glowed within her. She was very still for a moment, as Jillian floated over to the other side. Then her shoulders slumped slightly and her head fell forward as her eyes reopened. And to look in them was to know that the old Jillian was as dead as the man who had once been Spencer Armacost . . .

Postscript

Seven years later

It could have been a scene you might see anywhere in America. Two little boys—tow-headed identical twins who had passed their fifth birthdays and were well on their way to their sixth—walking down the driveway of their neat little suburban house.

Right behind them were their parents. The father was square-jawed, clear-eyed and his hair was brush-cut—just the look you expected of a man dressed in the flying suit of a pilot in the United States Air Force. His wings were embroidered on his chest, his captain's bars on his shoulders. His wife had dark hair and was petite and pretty—the former Jillian Armacost. She carried two paper bags, two identical lunches, and she tucked them into the pack each boy wore on his back.

"Ready for your first day of school?" Dad asked.

With a calm that suggested that the two little boys were older than their years, they answered: "Ready."

Their mother tapped the backpacks. "I gave you each an apple. And I want you to eat them. No trading, okay? Promise?"

Simultaneously the two little boys answered: "Promise."

A beep sounded and the little family looked up to see a bright yellow school bus pulled up to the curb. Stenciled on the side of the vehicle were the words: Nellis AFB Elementary School.

"There it is," Dad said.

"Give me a kiss," said Mom, kneeling down. Both boys kissed her on the cheek and Jillian held them tight. As the bus horn sounded again, the two kids broke from the embrace and raced across the lawn for the bus.

The two proud parents watched them go. "What do you think they'll be when they grow up?", Jillian asked.

Her husband laughed. "Grow up? Give them some time, honey. It's only their first day of school."

Jillian put her hands on his shoulders and turned him away from the school bus and the twins, then pulled him into a tender embrace.

She laid her head on his shoulder and watched as her boys stopped in front of the school bus door. They looked back over their shoulders at their mother.

"I think they are going to be pilots," she said softly. "Just like their father..."

"Stepfather," he said with an air of self-deprecation.

But Jillian did not appear to have heard him.

The twins were looking back at their mother. The sunny little-boy smiles gone now, as if their faces had been wiped blank and replaced with cold, dark, adult stares. Their eyes locked onto Jillian's for a moment, and mother and sons stared hard at each other for a moment as if joined in some wordless form of communication.

"I'm only their stepfather," the husband reiterated.

Jillian traced the embroidered wings sewn onto the chest of his flight overalls. "No," she said firmly. "You are their father now."

The bus horn beeped one more time and the link between Jillian and her twin sons snapped. There were smiles all round again, as if storm clouds had passed. The twins waved and clambered onto the school bus.

The twins knew most of the kids on the bus; they all lived near one another on the air force base. The other kids generally tried to make the ride to school a barely contained riot, but the twins seemed airily above it all. They walked to the very rear of the school bus and settled themselves in their seats. Each pulled a Walkman from his pack, plugged a pair of headphones into it and started the tape. As the sound reached their ears, the twins suddenly looked very peaceful, eerily so.

The shouts and yells of their schoolmates faded away as the twins listened to that terrible sound, growing louder as the seconds passed. It was as if it were sweet music in their ears . . .